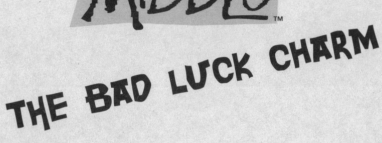

THE BAD LUCK CHARM

MALCOLM IN THE MIDDLE™

THE BAD LUCK CHARM

BY PAM POLLACK & MEG BELVISO

SCHOLASTIC INC.

New York   Toronto   London   Auckland   Sydney
Mexico City   New Delhi   Hong Kong

Based on the hit TV series created by Linwood Boomer.

ISBN 0-439-23078-0

12 11 10 9 8 7 6 5 4 3 2 1   1 2 3 5 6/0
Printed in the U.S.A.
First Scholastic printing, January 2001

THE BAD LUCK CHARM

My mom says we should be grateful for family. Sometimes that's really hard to do. Like last week, when we got burritos? I've done the math on how long a burrito should be in the microwave for a perfect mixture of melted core to chewy crust. So I should have been the one to set the timer on the microwave. But Reese decided it would be quicker if he set the microwave on high instead of medium without telling me. And Dewey was supposed to watch it and tell us if they started to smoke. But he got hypnotized watching the burritos go round and round on the tray. Me and Reese didn't even get to see the explosion, and since we didn't get to eat the burritos, we should have at least gotten to see them explode.

We got into a fight about it, and then Mom started yelling at us to clean the microwave, which was a bad idea. We started spraying one another with the soap and Dewey slipped on a burrito skin and said it was my fault, which it wasn't. It was Reese's fault for throwing the skin up to the ceiling to see if it would stick. Reese said it was Dewey's fault for being such a spaz.

Here's the bad part. My mom decided we need to learn to work together. Even if it kills us.

CHAPTER ONE

"**D**ewey, don't drink the maple syrup," Mom said.

My little brother's short blond hair was covered in the stuff and so was his face. I don't know how he does it.

I took the pitcher from Dewey and poured even more syrup on my blueberry-and-banana pancakes. Nobody makes better pancakes than Captain Buttermilk. That's our favorite restaurant to go to for breakfast on Sundays. They give us our own special table, way in the back, away from everyone. My brother Reese thinks it's because they respect our show of strength. I think it's because of the time we tried to do that trick where you pull the tablecloth off the table without pulling off the dishes? It didn't work, but it's still a good trick.

Reese took another pancake from the platter on the table. "Reese, how many pancakes have you had?" Mom asked incredulously.

"Eighteen," I answered for him. "Not including the silver-dollar one he sampled off the next table when the guy went to the bathroom."

Reese glared at me. "I'm in training," he said. "I need my carbs." He pushed up the sleeve of his sweatshirt to show me what he thought was a muscle.

"Reese, it's not a marathon, it's a Survivor Day. You have to use your brain to win," I pointed out.

"Maybe if you're a Krelboyne," Reese sneered.

The Krelboynes are the kids in this special genius class at my school. I got put into it this year and besides ruining my life, it's okay. We have our classes separate from the other kids, in a trailer by the tetherball court. But next Saturday, the whole school would be competing at Survivor Day. The idea is that we're given these challenges and we have to work as teams to win the event. Every event is worth points, and whichever team gets the most points is named Last of the Mohicans. I've been dreaming of winning Survivor Day since I was Dewey's age, the year Francis won it. He let me carry his trophy home for him. Reese is sure his team is going to win, but I know he's going down.

"So about this Survivor Day," Mom said. "I signed your permission slips."

"Excellent," said Reese with his mouth full and a piece of pancake in his spiky brown hair.

"And I filled in the names for the team you're going to be on."

Wait. What?

"Mom, we fill out that part ourselves," I explained. "I'm going to be on a team with Stevie."

Stevie is my best friend. He's a Krelboyne, too.

"Malcolm and Stevie the Wheelie," Reese snorted.

The piece of pancake fell out of his hair and onto his plate. "There's the team to beat."

"Shut up," I said.

"You're not beating my team," Reese said. "Every team member was handpicked after a killer tryout that I made up myself."

"You're on the same team," Mom announced.

Reese and I both stared at her. Her round brown eyes were totally serious.

"What's in these pancakes?" Dad asked, like he'd just noticed there was something in them.

"Blueberries and bananas, honey," Mom said. "You like them."

"Great," Dad said, going back to his breakfast.

"Mom," I said. "I can't be on a team with Reese. This is a battle of wits!"

"It's a battle of skills," Reese corrected me.

"I don't care what it is," said Mom. "You're in it together. It's about time you kids learned to appreciate that you have each other."

"Can I be on your team?" Dewey asked.

"No!" Me and Reese shouted together. We agreed on that much. Technically, Dewey wasn't even invited to Survivor Day. It was only for older kids like me and Reese.

"Mom, I promised Stevie we'd be on a team together," I said. "He's in a wheelchair." Mom knew Stevie was in a wheelchair, but I was playing on her sympathy here.

"You'll still be with Stevie," Mom said, like she

couldn't believe I'd said that. "I'm not going to kick that poor crippled boy off your team!"

"But, Mom, Malcolm and Stevie are Krelboynes," said Reese, like that should explain it.

"Why can't I be on your team?" Dewey whined. "I want to be on the team. I want it! I want it! I want it! I want it!"

"Look, Dewey," my dad said. "My pancake is in the shape of Florida."

Okay, that distracted Dewey for about a minute.

"Listen, you two," my mom said in her special tone of voice. The one that freezes you to your chair and makes you listen. "I am sick and tired of you fighting all the time. You're going to have to learn to get along sometime. If you want to be the Last of the Mohawks, you're going to have to rely on each other."

"Last of the Mohicans," I muttered.

"Good movie," said Dad.

Nobody said anything for a minute. That's not a good sign in our family. I was mad about being on Reese's team, Reese was mad about being on my team, and Dewey was mad about not being on any team.

"Yesterday," Dewey piped up, "Malcolm and Reese dropped me out of a tree."

I couldn't believe it. He promised he wouldn't tell. And anyway, we didn't drop him out of a tree. Well, we did, but he was in a sling so he fell really slowly.

"Shut up, you little dweeb," Reese warned, but the damage was pretty much done. Mom's eyes bugged out, and she started sucking in all the breath she would need to yell.

"Mom, we totally did not drop him out of a tree."

"Yeah," said Reese.

"We lowered him down in a sling. I tested it. It could hold him easily."

"The pantyhose were extra strength," said Reese.

"Right," I said. "There was a chart on the back. It said they could hold something three times Dewey's weight and double his size. We made sure before we tried it."

Here's the weird thing. Mom looked like she was getting madder the more we said about our safety tests. I couldn't figure out why. She's always telling us to be careful.

Mom's voice sounded like a train coming straight at us. And there was nowhere to run. "You ruined my new super control-top silk pantyhose!"

That got Dad's attention. "Oh, no," he said. "Not the hubba hubba heinies."

"I saw a monkey in the tree," said Dewey.

"You did not," said Reese. "Mom, the pantyhose are fine. They're not ripped or anything."

"They're probably just stretched out to the length of a tree," noted Dad. "Check, please."

Dewey sat between me and Reese on the ride home. He didn't want to. He knew the second me and Reese got him alone, he was dead meat. Our Sunday was ruined. Reese and I were going to spend the rest of the day being punished. Mom hadn't decided exactly what she was going to do to us yet. She was thinking about it. I think she was enjoying it because every few minutes she'd look at us from the front seat and smile.

"We're toast," Reese said.

"Stop the car!" Mom yelled suddenly.

Reese and I exchanged panicked looks. "Is she going to put us out on the street?" I whispered. Would she do that? That's against the law, isn't it?

"If you're thinking of leaving us here," said Reese, "we'll find our way home."

"No, silly," Mom said. "It's a tag sale!"

We stop at tag sales whenever we see them. You'd be surprised at the cool stuff some people get rid of. You'd also be surprised at the lame stuff some people have in their house. My dad pulled the car over, and we all got out. My mom grabbed me and Reese by the collars of our shirts. "You break it, you bought it," she warned us.

"This is so your fault," I said to Reese when Mom had gone over to a table full of bowls and plates. I don't know why she was looking at them. We have plenty of that stuff at home. Dewey was helping Dad look through some old records.

"Look for anything by Blue Oyster Cult, son," Dad advised him. Dad was singing to himself. "Don't fear the reaper ... baby, I'm your man."

"I don't know what her problem is," Reese said. "We tested those pantyhose like three times, and they were really strong."

8

"Yeah, and Dad's record collection is much heavier than Dewey."

"I can't believe I'm stuck with you and the Wheelie for Survivor Day," grumbled Reese. "Just remember I'm captain."

"No way, moron," I shot back.

"Yes way," said Reese. "I'm older and I'm the one with skills."

"What skills?" I said. "You can't even brush your teeth in the morning without getting toothpaste all over the sink."

Reese grabbed me. I grabbed Reese. We were about to hit the ground fighting . . . *and then we saw it.* It was sitting on a table all by itself.

The coolest dead monkey *ever!*

"I call it!" Reese and I both yelled, running over to the table. We each grabbed a bristly, hairy arm and started pulling.

"Let go!"

"It's mine!"

"Unhand that monkey!" a voice above us commanded. Reese and I stopped fighting and looked up. I swear he was the oldest man in the world. I didn't think people could get that old. Trees, maybe. But not people. The old old man took the scratchy monkey out of our hands and adjusted the little red jacket it wore. Then he fixed the little round hat on its head. The monkey's teeth were bared so you could see its fangs. It was stuffed — like the way they stuff a deer's head before mounting it on the wall — and its tail curled really stiff in the back. It had little twisted hands. The eyes had to be glass, but they looked alive. I could see stitches at the base of its head poking through the coarse monkey hair, where somebody had sewn up the skin. It was the most hideous thing ever. It was *so cool*.

The old man cradled the monkey like a baby and looked at us.

"So how much for the monkey?" Reese asked.

The old man glared down at us.

"This," he said in a gravelly voice. "This is not just a monkey. This is Banana Joe."

CHAPTER TWO

"**B**anana who?" Reese and I both said at the same time.

The old old man's nostrils flared. There was coarse hair in them like the monkey's. "Banana Joe," he repeated. "A name known on three continents and feared on just as many."

Reese and I looked at the monkey and back to the old old man. They kind of looked alike. Aside from the hair thing, they both had bony hands with yellow fingernails, wrinkly lips, and only one eyebrow that ran across their whole forehead.

"So how much?" Reese asked.

"Sit!" the old old man barked. Reese and I were so surprised, we sat down in two lawn chairs that were for sale behind us next to the pink flamingos. The old old man stood in front of us with the monkey casting a big shadow on the grass. "It was long ago and far away, in deepest Bomba-din."

"Gimme a break," Reese muttered.

The man glared at him and continued. "A card game was going on in an alley behind the marketplace. A poor merchant lost everything to a pitiless gambler with a thin mustache."

I glanced over to another table and saw Mom looking at a purple bean-bag chair while another woman looked over her shoulder.

"The merchant was forced to part with his most prized possession." The old old man held up Banana Joe.

"A dead monkey was his most prized possession?" Reese said. "That's pathetic." Reese held up two fingers at me to make an "L" for "Loser."

"The gambler thought as you did," the man snapped. "He stuffed Banana Joe in his trunk when he got on a steamer back to London from deepest Bomba-din."

"Look, mister," I interrupted. "My class just finished making an interactive map of the world out of modeling clay and rubber tubing. There is no such place as Bomba-din."

"Not anymore," he said ominously.

What was that supposed to mean?

"Halfway across the ocean," the old old man continued, "the steamer sprung a leak. One hundred and sixty-eight souls were lost. Among them, a foolish card shark who thought Banana Joe was just a monkey. He went down with the ship. Somehow Banana Joe made it to the lifeboats. No one knows how."

Reese and I rolled our eyes at each other. This guy had to be kidding. But I knew he was going to make us listen to more before he sold us the monkey. Mom and the lady who was looking over her shoulder were now both talking at once and pointing to the bean bag.

The old old man didn't notice them. Nothing would distract him from his long story. Was any monkey worth this?

I looked at Banana Joe. His teeth were sharp and kind of yellow. Yeah, he was worth it. You know who would really love this monkey? My brother Francis. He's away at military school. He didn't want to be sent to military school. He kind of got framed. Every time something blew up in our family, it got blamed on Francis. It wasn't fair.

The old old man cleared his throat. "The lifeboat was rescued by a ship they called *The Golden Antelope*," he said. "The *Antelope* captain found Banana Joe and took him home to his son. The next day when his father went to wake him up for breakfast, the boy was gone. Only the monkey remained in the bed, curled up with the boy's teddy bear."

"Where did the boy go?" I asked, trying not to sound creeped out.

The old old man narrowed his watery eyes. "Nobody knows," he said. "Certainly not his family. They never saw him again."

"Oh, *man!*" Reese said, grinning. "We have *got* to have this monkey. It's the ultimate in Dewey-control. One look at this monkey and the little blabbermouth is ours for life!"

"Quiet!" the old old man bellowed. For a second, everyone looked over. Except Mom and the lady. They were nose to nose over the bean-bag chair.

"What's this guy's problem?" Reese mumbled to me.

"Don't question it," I said. "The sooner he finishes, the sooner we get the monkey."

Reese and I tried to look really interested in how the story turned out. The old old man seemed to like that. Banana Joe didn't look like he was buying it, though. I think he knew we were just pretending to get what we wanted. Wait. He didn't know anything. He's a dead monkey. What am I talking about?

"After the mysterious disappearance of his son, the captain left the monkey alone on the London docks, sitting on an orange crate. Nothing was heard about him for years until he turned up in a circus side-show traveling right near here. I was six years old the first time I saw Banana Joe. He spoke to me. He was ready to leave the circus."

This was getting even weirder. Reese looked confused.

The old old man continued. "I waited until Mr. Electrico was all charged up and ready to light a lamp with his tongue, and then I freed Joe from his captors and took him home. He's lived with me ever since."

At this point I was wondering which one was creepier, him or the monkey. I added up all the factors and decided it was a tie. This is going to sound weird, but I could swear the monkey was listening to the story, too. It was like, he liked hearing about himself.

"All these years Banana Joe has stood by me. My enemies are his enemies. But now it's time for him to leave me and let the Banana Joe saga continue."

"Why?" I asked.

The old old man glared. "They're putting me in a retirement home, and they won't let me bring him. They said he frightens the other old people."

We waited a second. We couldn't believe he was finally finished. Then Reese said, "Okay, how much do you want for him?"

"Sixty-eight cents."

"Deal," said Reese, digging into his pocket.

The old man put the monkey in a brown paper bag, and handed it to me. I know it sounds stupid, but I was afraid this monkey was going to start talking to me now. I peeked into the bag. He didn't. He just grinned up at me like a dead monkey.

"Let's go," Reese said.

We both turned around and stepped right into a brown puddle. Which so *wasn't* there before. I'm not even going to think about what it was a puddle of. I looked back in the bag and the monkey was still grinning at me. As I looked into his eyes, I heard a shriek.

"Get your paws off that bean bag, lady!"

My mom was seriously yelling at the other lady by the bean-bag chair. The other lady made the mistake of trying to argue, and then Mom really let her have it.

"You didn't even *want* that bean-bag chair until you saw me looking at it. Well, get over it, I'm taking it!" Mom picked up the chair and squashed it to her chest. "Boys!" she yelled so that people three tag sales away could hear her. "We're going home!"

Mom marched across the lawn with the bean-bag chair. It was really hard to hold, because it kept sliding through her arms like she was holding a blob of purple jelly. The other lady ran after her, yelling at Mom to stop. Mom turned around and body-checked her with the bean-bag chair. It was awesome. Mom thought so, too, because she kept doing it. The other lady kept bouncing off her like a superball.

Finally, Dad came up and grabbed Mom, swinging her around toward the car. The other lady grabbed onto the chair and pulled. There was a ripping sound. The chair sprung a leak. Suddenly, little beads were pouring out of it. Dad kept pushing Mom to the car while the other lady screamed. It was probably time to go now.

Reese and I turned back to the old old man. He was gone. I'm sure there's a reasonable explanation for that. I just don't know it right now. Reese grabbed the bag away from me. We ran to the car and climbed inside. Dewey was already there, holding something in his lap.

"Dewey, what did you buy?" Reese asked as Dad started the car.

"It's a dune buggy," Dewey said.

"No it's not," said Reese. "It's a Barbie Beach Buggy, moron. It says so right on the side."

"It is not!" said Dewey. "It's a dune buggy like the one Water Man rides when he's not in the water."

"Dewey," I said. "When Water Man isn't in the water, he has to wear an oxygen suit. And he would never drive anything pink."

"Boys, leave your brother alone," Mom said. "You guys are in enough trouble as it is."

"Don't fear the reaper . . ." Dad sang softly behind the wheel. There were beans from the dead bean bag in the collar of his dark green polo shirt.

Reese smiled evilly at Dewey and squeezed the brown paper bag. I swear I saw something move inside the bag. But it was just my imagination, right?

"Dewey," Reese said with a twinkle in his eye. "We got you a new friend."

Dewey had known Reese long enough to know that whatever was in that bag was not his friend. He tried to squeeze over to me like he hadn't gotten *me* in trouble at breakfast.

"You'd better be careful around your new friend," I whispered to Dewey. "He sort of has magic powers. And if he wants to, he can make bad things happen."

There was a funny noise, like the car was going over lots of bumps all of a sudden.

"Don't tell me," said Mom.

"Flat tire," said Dad.

"I can't believe it," Mom groaned as Dad pulled to the side of the road.

"What can I say?" Dad said. "Bad things happen."

Okay, I know it was just a coincidence. But just the same, the whole time Dad was fixing the tire? I was thinking about that sinking steamer from deepest Bomba-din.

CHAPTER THREE

When we got home, we went straight to our room. We made sure Dewey came with us. Even a twisted, wrinkle-faced monkey with glass eyes couldn't make us forget that Dewey had totally ratted us out at breakfast for ruining Mom's pantyhose. Now he was going to pay. I shut the door and Reese backed Dewey up against the wall. "You've got a big mouth," Reese said.

Dewey shut his mouth tight.

"I'll bet you think you really got us back," I said.

Dewey nodded.

"Reese, show him the monkey."

Reese pulled Banana Joe out of the brown paper bag and held him nose to nose with Dewey. The monkey's nostrils were the size of jumbo grapes. Dewey whined and covered his eyes. "It's scary! Take it away!"

"Dewey," Reese said. "This is Banana Joe. He's going to be living in our room from now on. He doesn't like squealers."

Reese and I told Dewey the history of Banana Joe. Well, we told him our version of the story, which was better than the one we'd heard from the old old man. In our version, there were at least twelve little boys who'd disappeared because they ratted someone out. And they never saw their families again. There was a good chance they were taken away by monsters and had to live in a cage. And there was a mummy. Reese just threw that in because Dewey's afraid of mummies.

When we were finished, Dewey had curled up in a ball on the floor, moaning. Reese was poking him with Banana Joe's shriveled finger and saying, "Dewey, you'd better not tell on us. You'd better not tell . . ."

Dewey tried to roll under the bed, but I played goalie and pushed him back into play.

"Stop! Stop!" Dewey said.

We just kept poking him.

"I'm going to pee!"

We stopped poking him. We'd known Dewey long enough to know he wasn't kidding. When Dewey ran to the bathroom, Reese straightened Banana Joe's jacket.

"Worth every penny," he declared, tossing him on the bed. He bounced off the stock cars on the bedspread and rolled onto the pillow.

I ran over and picked him up. "Don't just toss him like that."

"What's your problem?" Reese asked. "He's just a stuffed animal."

Reese had a point. But then, that gambler had a

point, too, and now he sleeps with the fishes. And he's no Water Man.

"I just don't want him to get messed up," I said.

Reese frowned at me suspiciously. He knew I was lying and he was trying to figure out why. I could hear his brain working. Then he got it. "You're afraid of the monkey!"

"Am not!" I yelled.

Reese picked up the toy and waved its dried-up arms in the air. "He's coming to get you, Malcolm," he said. "He wants your brain for his monkey head!" Reese moved closer and stuck the monkey's claws into my hair shouting, "Brains! Brains! Brains!"

"Quit it!" I yelled, pushing Reese away.

Banana Joe fell on the floor. I ducked down and ran headfirst into Reese's stomach. Reese grunted and wrestled me to the ground. I was face-to-face with Banana Joe, and he was looking at me. I don't know why he was looking at me. Reese was the one who threw him on the floor. "Aaaaagggh!" I yelled, pushing Reese off me and falling on top of him. We didn't even hear Mom's footsteps in the hall.

"Boys!" she yelled, pulling us apart. "All right, get into the hallway and —" Mom's eyes got wide. Me and Reese followed her look down to the floor, where Banana Joe's shriveled hand was poking out from under the bed. "Oh, my god!" Mom screamed. "What did you do to your brother?"

"Mom, that's not Dewey," I said. "It's Banana Joe." Reese went over and picked him up. "See?"

Mom looked at our new monkey. "That's the most hideous thing I've ever seen," she declared.

"I know," I said. "Isn't it great?"

"Malcolm's scared of it," said Reese.

"Am not."

"Where did you get that thing?" Mom asked. "And please tell me it was dead when you got it."

"We bought it at the tag sale," I said.

"It was while you were terminating that bean bag," said Reese.

"I did not terminate anything, mister," Mom said. Leave it to Reese to bring up a really bad subject right before we're going to get punished. "I saw that bean bag first. That's the law of the tag sale. You break the law, you pay the price. Which reminds me. You two. Out in the hallway. *Now*."

As Mom shoved us out of the room, I saw the bathroom door open. Dewey poked his head out. When he saw it was all clear, he came back into our room.

Two hours later, Reese and I were kneeling with our faces to the wall and our hands clasped behind our heads. "As much as this stinks," Reese said, "it's good training for Survivor Day."

I turned my cheek to the wall to look at him for a second. "Oh, yeah, right," I said. "I can just see this as one of the events at Survivor Day. Canoeing, racing, and staring at a wall for two hours."

"Endurance is key," said Reese. "That's what Sensei Scott down at the Y says."

"Oh, well, in that case, we're sure to win," I said, turning back to the wall.

"I don't think it's fair I'm getting punished twice," Reese said. "It's bad enough I have to have you and your Krelboyne friend on my team."

"It's not your team," I reminded him. "Me and Stevie already had a team. It's *our* team."

"I'm the one with natural leadership abilities," Reese bragged.

"You're the one who led us here, Sensei Reese, right into a wall."

"It was your idea to use the pantyhose to lower Dewey out of that tree," Reese said.

"Only because your idea was to drop Dewey out of the tree holding an umbrella."

"It works like a parachute," Reese said impatiently.

"Only in cartoons," I said, raising my eyes to the ceiling. "If you're not Bugs Bunny, you fall to your death."

"Whatever."

How was I supposed to work with this guy on Survivor Day? We were going to be the First of the Mohicans to get picked off by the competition. It was so unfair.

Mom came out and told us we could get up. While we waited for the blood to come back into our arms, we walked into the kitchen where Dad was reading the paper and tapping on two half empty juice glasses with a pencil.

"Dewey tells me you have a monkey," Dad said, looking at us from over his glasses. There was a kind of spark in his eyes, and they crinkled up in the corners.

Reese and I looked at each other: What did Dad know? He pushed a plate of Oreo cookies toward us. We pulled some apart and started licking the creamy centers.

"Dewey claims your monkey eats kids. Let's talk about that," said Dad. "Have you actually seen this monkey eat any kids, or is it just neighborhood gossip?"

Me and Reese laughed. We told him about the old old man and the weird story he told us and how we got the monkey for sixty-eight cents.

"Which was sixty-eight more cents than he paid for it," Reese said. "He took it from a carnival."

"But only because Banana Joe wanted to leave," said Dad. "He wanted to be with people who respected him. Everyone knows that about Banana Joe."

Wait. What did he mean "everyone knows"? Who had ever heard of Banana Joe besides us?

"You know about Banana Joe?" I asked.

"Sure," said Dad. "Banana Joe is right up there with the boogeyman, that guy with the hook, Jack the Ripper. He's one of the greats. You're braver than I am, son, sleeping with him in your room."

Reese and I looked at each other, trying to figure out if Dad was kidding.

"You know the Banana Joe story that scared me the most?" Dad said. "One Halloween a kid stole the monkey for a prank. Well, anyone knows that you never use Banana Joe for a joke. If you don't respect him, he'll get you. Just like he got that kid. I've never been able to look at a pitchfork the same way again."

Dad shuddered.

"They found his UNICEF box on the ground beside him. He'd collected sixty-eight cents." Dad shook his head sadly, like he really missed that kid.

"Come on, Dad, you can't really believe in that stuff?" I asked.

Dad hesitated, then he smiled. "Of course not, Malcolm. It's just a legend." He didn't sound very convincing.

"So . . . what are you telling us?" said Reese. "That we've got a psycho monkey in our room?"

Dad shrugged. "I'm just telling you the way I heard it. When you don't respect the monkey, bad things happen. Very bad things."

Sometimes my dad can be really cool. Like when he gets us out of school to take us to the stock car races? Or when he distracts Mom when she's about to yell at us? Or when we go on long car trips and he makes up games to play and gets us to sing "The Banana Boat Song" together. "Daay-aay-o!"

But, you know, dads are supposed to tell you there's no such thing as the boogeyman. They're definitely not supposed to tell you the stuffed monkey you just bought might come after you with a pitchfork.

But my dad has never been like other dads. When I was little, I told my dad there was a monster under my bed. He told me I should feed it raw meat. Now he was telling me I should watch my back around a tag sale special.

Not that I believe him. I'm not Dewey, right? But that doesn't mean I want Banana Joe sitting right next to my face while I'm sleeping, which is where Reese wanted to put him. I said we should put him on Reese's side of the room. Reese tried to put Joe in bed with me. I hit Reese with my pillow. Then I rolled over on the hairy beast, and he bit me. I mean, I cut my finger on his sharp tooth. Reese said Joe did it on purpose. I told him to shut up.

Dewey said he was scared of the monkey monster. So we put the monkey monster on the dresser right across from Dewey and turned off the light.

CHAPTER FOUR

When I woke up Monday morning, the first thing I noticed was Dewey squatting like a monkey on the floor in front of Banana Joe. "Dewey, what are you doing?" I asked.

Dewey didn't answer me. But he did talk to Joe.

"What's your favorite kind of ice cream?" Dewey asked Joe. He waited a second. "Mine, too," he said. "That and Oregon blackberry."

I sat up and stared at him. Reese sat up in his bed, too. "Who are you talking to, you little weirdo?"

"That's my brother Reese," Dewey explained, as if the stuffed animal had asked who had spoken. "The one I told you about."

Reese and I looked at each other and then got out of bed. We kneeled on either side of Dewey. "Dewey," I said. "You shouldn't bother Banana Joe. You might make him mad. You know what happens when he gets mad, don't you?"

"He's not mad," Dewey said matter-of-factly. "He's nice. We're friends now. We climbed a tree and then we had Slurpees."

"You did not," said Reese.

"Banana Joe doesn't like you," Dewey said. "He told me."

"He did not!" Reese said. He sounded a little nervous. Even if you know a stuffed monkey isn't alive, you still don't want to hear it doesn't like you.

"Banana Joe says you're a big meanie bottom," Dewey announced.

Banana Joe sounded suspiciously like Dewey himself. Meanie bottom?

"Banana Joe says meanie bottoms get put in the garbage can."

Reese grabbed Dewey by the front of his pajamas, twisting the face of the happy dinosaur printed on them. "Listen, you little twerp," he threatened. "One more word and you're so dead."

Dewey glanced over at Banana Joe and then back at Reese. "Now Banana Joe really doesn't like you."

I really wished Dewey would cut that out. I didn't like feeling like there was a fourth person in the room with us. A fourth person with curled fingernails and yellow teeth.

"That's totally stupid," Reese said. "Of course he likes me. I own him. He's, like, my slave."

Dewey looked really scared now. He looked back at the bristly hairs on Banana Joe's chin and then twisted out of Reese's grip. "No! No!" Dewey cried. "Take it back! You're making Banana Joe angry! Take it back!"

Dewey ran into the bathroom and shut the door.

"Dewey, come out," I said through the door. "It's just a stupid monkey."

"Don't say that," he wailed. "Banana Joe is going to get you. Just like he's going to get Reese."

"This is so lame," Reese said to me. "Dewey, you're not scaring me. Get out of the bathroom."

"Reese, I don't think he's trying to scare us," I said. "He's really lost it this time."

Reese considered that possibility. "Cool," he said.

We got dressed for school. We had to use Mom and Dad's bathroom because Dewey wouldn't get out of ours until we were almost late. I didn't like that thing in the little red jacket watching me while I was getting dressed, so I turned it around to face the wall.

"Dude, I can't believe you're really scared of it," Reese said. "You're supposed to have a brain."

"Reese, I'm not scared of a stupid stuffed toy," I said. That was kind of a lie. I knew I was being ridiculous, but I still didn't want that thing looking at me in my underwear.

"I can't believe I get stuck with a total wimp on my team for Survivor Day. You're an embarrassment!"

I grabbed Banana Joe and turned him around again so he was facing me. Then I spun to face Reese. "There, are you happy?" I said. "I told you I am not afraid of the stupid monkey. Ow!"

I couldn't believe it. One of the hairy ape's claws was stuck in my shirt and poked me in the back. "Cut it out!" I yelled at Banana Joe.

When I looked back at Reese, he was shaking his head. "Dude, seriously," he said. "Get some help."

Reese walked into the kitchen, leaving me alone and feeling like an idiot. I may not be the toughest guy in the world, but I'd never been afraid of an inanimate object before. As much as I hate to say it, Reese had a point about me being an embarrassment. I thought I'd totally prepared for Survivor Day. I'd secretly been doing pushups in the bathtub and I'd even watched one of Reese's tapes: *When Animals Attack . . . How to Fight Back*. I already had a knapsack packed with everything I needed stowed away in the closet. But how could I have prepared for this?

It was my turn to walk Dewey to school. When I ran back into my room to get my books, I noticed something in front of Banana Joe. There were six Pez candies in four different colors lined up at his feet. Oh, great, now Dewey was leaving him offerings. I had to have a talk with him.

We walked past a lot of houses that looked like ours, only neater. As we got to the corner of our block, I said, "You're not fooling anybody with that monkey act you know."

"Did you know Banana Joe likes rocky road ice cream?" Dewey said.

"Dewey, he can't eat ice cream. He can't eat anything."

Dewey just shrugged and kept walking. I decided to try a different tactic. One way or another I was going to find out what was really going on.

"So what do you and Banana Joe talk about?" I asked.

Dewey started babbling. "He tells me stories. Once there was this boy. He was mean to his brother. He was mean to Banana Joe. Banana Joe didn't like him. The boy was sorry. Very sorry."

"What did he do to him?"

I had to ask, didn't I?

"He gave him to the garbage man," Dewey answered, like that made any sense at all. "And then the mice ate him. Except his ears."

Why did I think I was going to feel better after talking to Dewey? I could almost believe he was talking to Banana Joe. And that Banana Joe was talking back.

CHAPTER FIVE

Every Monday morning in my class, we do this thing called "the brainstorm." One person picks a topic and the whole class talks about it. Last week it was Dabney's turn. He wanted to talk about fungus. The week before that we talked about how bears go to the bathroom when they're hibernating (they don't!).

This week it was my turn. When math was over, we all moved our chairs into a circle. I put my chair next to my friend Stevie's wheelchair. We were sitting in front of the glass tank full of frogs. We try not to get too attached to our frogs, because we're going to be dissecting them later in the year.

"You're . . . up," said Stevie, looking at me through his thick glasses. He always talks that way. He needs to take a separate breath for each word. It takes a while for him to say what he has to say, but it's usually worth it.

"Malcolm?" my teacher said. "Anything you want to talk about?"

I was planning on talking about this time when Reese accidentally sat on a hot plate when we were little and he got this giant blister on his butt cheek

33

and weird colored stuff started coming out of it. I always wanted to know why that was.

But that would have to wait until next time. Today belonged to Banana Joe. "Does anyone here believe in bad luck charms? Like, if something has a curse on it, and you buy it, it could put a curse on you?"

A kid in my class named Martin Stephens studied me seriously. I studied his freckles. Sometimes you could see constellations on his nose. "Everyone feels cursed sometimes," Martin said. "It's all in your head."

That wasn't much help.

"I'm not talking about that," I said. "I'm talking about a thing that brings bad luck to the person who has it."

"You . . . mean . . . like . . . the . . . curse . . . on . . . King . . . Tut's . . . tomb?" Stevie asked.

"There was a curse on King Tut's tomb?" I asked.

That was weird, because we were working on making a model of King Tut's tomb in our classroom out of Lincoln Logs and tinfoil.

"Oh . . . yeah," said Stevie. "Everyone . . . who . . . went . . . inside . . . died."

"Nonsense," said Eraserhead. "Of course, they died. They were breathing bad tomb air. It's completely scientific."

"Not . . . scientific," breathed Stevie. "Sacred . . . ground . . . powerful . . . stuff."

"They breathed tomb spores," Eraserhead insisted.

"I'm allergic to spores," Flor said. "They make my head swell up."

"Okay, what about a sporeless curse," I said. "What if you buy something weird and everyone who owned it before you had bad things happen to them, like right after they bought it?"

"Why would anyone buy that?" Flor said.

"Because it was really cool," I snapped. "And it was sixty-eight cents."

"Well, if you're going to do something like that," Eraserhead said. "*I* can't help you. You're just asking for trouble."

That made me mad. "What happened to tomb spores?" I said. "I thought you didn't believe in curses."

"I don't," said Eraserhead. "But I don't go around buying hexed objects, either."

"I'm not allowed to buy hexed objects," Dabney said. "I had a lucky marble once. My mom made me throw it out."

"What you're forgetting," Martin said, "is that the mind is a very powerful thing. If you expect bad luck, you're going to get it. You psych yourself out."

"But what if you don't think you believe in this stuff, but then stuff starts happening anyway?" I asked.

"Then . . . you're . . . in . . . trouble," Stevie said.

I tried to act like I believed what Martin said about psyching yourself out. I walked outside to the lunch tables with Stevie rolling beside me. "Okay, from now on I'm not going to expect any bad luck," I said. "There's no reason anything bad should happen to me. So it won't."

That was simple, wasn't it?

I took two more steps, and then my lunch bag was knocked out of my hand onto the ground and stomped on. It was peanut butter and jelly. I saw it oozing out of the squashed bag. I looked up into the face of Doug Sligo, our school bully. He has beady little eyes in a big doughy face, kind of like an evil, uncooked gingerbread man.

"Looks like it's your lucky week," Sligo jeered, breathing into my face. He had peanut butter for lunch, too. "I'm making sure everybody gets what they deserve. I'm going alphabetically, so I don't miss anyone. This week it's your turn."

Sligo lumbered back over to his goons, who were cheering and laughing. One was skinny and tall, and the other was short and solid like a block. This is what I had to look forward to all week. "So much for psyching yourself out," I said. Banana Joe had been in my life for one day, and I had a whole week of bad luck already guaranteed. Who knew Sligo knew the alphabet?

Stevie ate his lunch, and I listened to my stomach growl. Stevie offered to share his tofu-and-mung-bean sandwich with me, but I figured the air in my mouth tasted better than that, so I said no. I wanted to tell him about Banana Joe, but first I had to tell him the other bad news about Reese being on our team for Survivor Day. Reese was playing football with some other kids on the playground, and everyone else was watching.

"Your . . . brother . . . is . . . excellent," Stevie said as Reese plowed into another kid and got the ball.

"I'm glad you think so," I said. "Because my mom says me and Reese have to be on the same team for Survivor Day."

Stevie turned and stared at me. His eyes got huge behind his glasses. "You're . . . kidding."

"My mom never kids about stuff like this. She thinks we need to learn to work together or something. I think we're just going to kill each other."

"What . . . about . . . me?"

"She signed you up on our team, too. Now Reese thinks he's the captain."

Stevie watched as Reese slammed into another kid and knocked him flat. "Oh . . . no."

While Stevie was still watching the body count rise in the football game, I told him all about my other problem. The one named Banana Joe. Stevie didn't tell me I was crazy. That was a good sign.

"All I know is that things have been weird since we brought that monkey home. I mean, it was the perfect plan to get Dewey back for telling on us. And it's a really cool monkey. You should see it. It's got sharp teeth and claws and wrinkled hands and it smells like chemicals? It should have been the best thing we ever bought."

"Except . . . for . . . the . . . curse," said Stevie.

"Yeah," I said. "That's the problem. How was I supposed to know there was real bad luck attached to this thing? The guy who sold it to us didn't even know there was no such place as Bomba-din."

"Not . . . anymore," said Stevie with a smile.

I ignored that.

"Okay, I admit it. I didn't respect the monkey. Just like the gambler didn't respect the monkey, and he drowned. Just like the sea captain didn't respect the monkey, and his kid disappeared. Just like that boy didn't respect the monkey, and he ended up on a pitchfork. According to Dewey, Banana Joe is going to get me. But what am I supposed to do about it?"

"Bury . . . it," said Stevie.

"What?" I said. "You mean like in the backyard?"

"No," said Stevie. "Must . . . be . . . sacred . . . ground."

"Says who?" I asked. "Since when did you become an expert on cursed object removal?"

"Always," he said. "I've . . . read . . . every . . . Tales . . . From . . . the . . . Crypt . . . comic . . . Always . . . bury . . . in . . . sacred . . . ground . . . Otherwise . . . they . . . come . . . back."

"Come back?" I asked. "How could it unbury itself? It's not like it can move."

"What . . . about . . . the . . . lifeboat?"

"Okay, nobody knows how Banana Joe got out of the gambler's trunk and into the lifeboat. But that doesn't mean we're living in a *Tales From the Crypt* comic. If I really wanted to get rid of that shrunken ape, I could just throw him away. I'm not looking all over for sacred ground."

"You'll . . . be . . . sorry," warned Stevie.

"Shut up!" I said. Why did everyone keep telling me I'd be sorry?

I turned around to the football game, where Reese had just intercepted the ball. Everyone cheered, especially Wendy Finnerman. She's this girl in Reese's class that he really likes.

Reese didn't respect Banana Joe, either, and he totally wasn't worried about bad luck. He waved at Wendy and motioned toward the goal, like he was going to score a touchdown just for her or something.

Reese started to run with the ball, leaving everyone else behind. As he neared the goal a little girl who looked like she was in kindergarten ran out at him from the crowd, like she was going to tackle him.

The little girl took a running leap—and knocked Reese flat! She got on his chest and shook her fists in victory. Then she picked up the football and scored a touchdown. The crowd watched in stunned silence. Finally Reese sat up. That's when the crowd started laughing.

"Did that mean little girl hurt you, Reese?" somebody jeered.

"That's why kindergartners shouldn't play football," a guy on Reese's team said, laughing.

He meant Reese was the kindergartner.

Reese went pale.

"Sacred ... ground," Stevie repeated. "Sacred ... ground."

CHAPTER SIX

That night I found Reese sitting on the washing machine with his infrared binoculars, looking out the window. "What are you doing?" I asked.

"Keeping watch," he said.

"For who?"

"Them," he said. "My enemies. They're out there. They smell opportunity. They think I'm down, but they're in for a surprise. I'm ready for them."

The worst thing about this? Was that I didn't even get to enjoy Reese being totally humiliated. It just made me think about Banana Joe.

"Reese, nobody cares that a little girl tackled you. It's not a big deal."

Reese looked at me like I was crazy, and I didn't blame him. Of course, it was a big deal. I would die if that ever happened to me. But I thought Reese could take it. As long as he can beat someone up, he doesn't care what they think of him. People don't laugh at Reese for long.

"Can I ask you something, like, seriously?" said Reese.

I nodded.

"You don't think that thing from the tag sale had something to do with this, do you?"

That was just what I didn't want to hear. I knew he wasn't talking about Barbie's Beach Buggy. "Reese, that's impossible," I said. I hoped I sounded convincing. "It was just an accident. She got in a lucky shot. It's not like you were on TV or something. Outside of the playground, nobody even knows about it."

"Yeah, right," said Reese. He still looked skeptical, but I could see he wanted to believe me.

"I'm telling you, Reese, nobody knows about it. And even if they did, they wouldn't care."

Reese frowned at the window again. "I can still see their faces," he growled.

Reese had really lost it. But when my dad came into the room a minute later, I could see their faces, too. Because my dad had the same expression.

Dad took a deep breath, like it was painful to remember.

"Hey, Reese," he said, coming into the room. "I heard you had a little trouble today with a really mean little girl." Dad looked at Reese sadly.

Reese turned a greenish color. His mouth opened, but no sound came out.

"What?" I said. I couldn't believe it. How did Dad know what happened at school? "Where did you hear about it?"

Dad straightened up. "The guy at the car wash told

me. Well, he mimed it because he doesn't really speak English."

"That's it," declared Reese. "I'm going to military school with Francis." Reese slid off the washing machine. "I'm going to pack."

Dad caught him at the door. "Son, son," he said. "I know this seems like a big deal now, but it's things like this that make the man."

Reese shook his head. "I'm history in this town. There's nothing for me here, now." He started to walk into our room, but Dad looked him right in the eye.

"Young man, let me tell you about another boy who felt that way."

From the way Dad was talking, I knew he was about to tell us a story that was supposed to inspire us but probably wouldn't. He had dozens of them. Like the story of the kid who lost all his fingers sticking his hand out the car window and went on to become the voice of Tippy the Tuna on TV. Or Earl the Spelling Cowboy who overcame a fear of horses and words beginning with c-h-l. But most of Dad's stories turned out to be really about Dad. He just didn't tell us until the end. Reese and I sighed. There's no stopping Dad when he wants to tell one of these stories.

"It was at the Roller Boogie skating championship. This young man was poised to take home the golden wheel. And then right in the middle of a triple-axle spin to 'Stairway to Heaven,' the elastic in his skating pants snapped. He didn't notice until he tripped over them and went sliding across the rink, picking up several splinters in unfortunate places. Ouch."

"Dad, why are you telling us this?" I moaned.

"Because that boy didn't give up! He finished the routine. I'm telling you, boys, the audience was in tears. In the face of utter humiliation, he was a true hero."

"Yeah, Dad," said Reese impatiently. "And that boy was you, right?"

Dad blinked. "What?" he said. "Oh, God, no. Nothing like that ever happened to me. I became state champion three years in a row."

Why does my dad always do this to us?

"So what happened to the other boy?" I demanded. "The one whose pants fell down?"

"Oh, him?" Dad said. "Nobody knows what happened to him. He disappeared. Probably from shame. But I don't think he ever got tackled by a kindergartner."

Reese dropped his head onto the washing machine with a loud thump.

Dad looked concerned. He led us into the kitchen. "Come on, I'll make you my famous bologna Oreos."

I had to admit that bologna Oreos sounded really good right now. I followed Dad and Reese into the kitchen. Dewey was sitting at the table picking out

Lucky Charms from the box, so he had one of each shape. I just knew they were for Banana Joe.

"Banana Joe still doesn't like Reese," he said as we came in.

"Shut up, you little dweeb," Reese said.

"Reese is a little upset," Dad told Dewey.

"Banana Joe says Reese isn't nice to him," Dewey said.

"I am so!" yelled Reese.

"Dewey, shut up," I said.

Dad patted Dewey on the head. "Don't be silly, Dewey," he said. "I'm sure Reese and Malcolm are both very nice to Banana Joe. They know what the monkey's capable of."

Me and Reese looked at each other uncomfortably.

"You do respect the monkey, don't you, boys?" Dad asked.

That's it. I'd had it. "It's a dead monkey!" I yelled. "I don't have to respect it or feed it Lucky Charms or take it out for ice cream. It's an inanimate object. It can't do anything to me."

I heard myself and I didn't sound like I believed myself.

"Of course, it can't, Malcolm," Dad said. He didn't sound so sure, either. "Nothing bad has ever happened to anyone because they weren't nice to a scraggly stuffed monkey."

I relaxed a little.

"Except for that one kid," Dad continued. Dad

never knew when to quit. "Liked to play practical jokes. Had sixty-eight cents in his pocket when they found him. They needed three coffins to bury him."

Neither of us finished our bologna Oreos after Dad's little story. Reese went back to watching out the window with his infrared goggles. Me? I called Francis.

"What's up?" Francis asked when he came to the phone. "Did you convince Mom and Dad to write a letter getting me out of the nature hike because of my fear of nature?"

"What?" I said. I'd almost forgotten about that. "Yeah, no problem. I told them you wanted to work on your science report instead. You're writing about the mating habits of fruit flies."

"Got it," said Francis. "Malcolm, you're my man. I don't know what I'd do without you. You can handle anything."

Did Francis really think I could handle anything? Was I going to tell him how not true that was? Was I going to tell him that I couldn't even handle an inanimate object with teeth?

No, I wasn't going to tell him that. I hung up the phone leaving Francis thinking I was the man. I'd rather face the beast in my room than have Francis think I was some little kid who believed in bristly haired shriveled-up monkey monsters.

Dewey was already asleep when Reese and I went to bed. I kept my back to the monkey while I put on my pajamas. I hoped Reese wouldn't notice. Luckily, tonight, he was doing the same thing.

"If anybody laughs at me tomorrow, I'll kill them," Reese said after I turned off the light.

It was good to hear Reese sounding like a happy thug again. I turned over and tried to go to sleep . . . but I couldn't. I lay there in the dark knowing Banana Joe was across the room behind me, smiling with his wrinkled lips. But what if he wasn't? What if I turned around and the beast was right next to me? What if I didn't turn around and the evil demon ape snuck up on me without me knowing it?

I turned around. I could see the shape of the monkey on the dresser, just where we'd left him. His eyes were kind of glowing? Which was probably because there was moonlight shining on them. If there was a moon tonight. I really hoped there was a moon tonight.

I kept looking at the thing on the dresser, and the thing on the dresser kept looking back. I closed my eyes, but he kept his open. I could feel them looking at me.

Okay, this was ridiculous. I'm terrified of a sixty-eight-cent yard-sale monkey. I knew it was stupid but I couldn't help it. I could either get up and move the monkey or I could not sleep again for the rest of my life. If I sleep eight hours a night, three hundred and sixty-five days a year, and I live seventy more years, that means I'm going to spend 204,400 hours staring at this miniature gorilla in the dark. I don't think so.

I slipped out of bed and tiptoed over to Banana Joe. I didn't really want to touch him, but I picked him up and moved him about two feet over. Then I turned it so that it was looking right at Reese instead of me.

That shouldn't have made me feel better, but it did. When I crawled back into bed, I fell right to sleep.

When I woke up, sun was streaming in the window, and the birds were singing. And Banana Joe was looking right at me again.

Okay, I admit it. I'm a little scared.
Don't get me wrong, I still don't think
Banana Joe is alive. He can just humil-
iate Reese, make Dewey his slave,
and move around by himself at night.
No big deal.

I'll bet Mom could handle Banana Joe.
I could just see her. "Listen mister,"
she'd tell the monkey. "You just think
of all the monkeys that don't have
organ grinder's hats and Lucky Charms
cereal the next time you decide to
curse someone. Otherwise I'll give you
such a haircut, people will be calling
you Banana Peel!"

That would be great.

But I can't tell Mom about this. We'd
look like complete idiots. This is something me and Reese have to handle
ourselves. And we're not too good at
working together.

CHAPTER SEVEN

I was hoping Sligo had forgotten he was supposed to be tormenting me all week. The guy can't remember to take a shower once a week. How can he remember which kid he's scheduled to pummel?

It turns out that he can. As I was walking toward the Krelboyne trailer before school, the tetherball came flying out of nowhere and hit me in the head, so I fell down and dropped all my books at Sligo's feet. That sent Sligo into a fit of laughter. Then a squirrel ran away with my math homework. At lunch, Sligo grabbed my bologna sandwich and licked it on both sides and then gave it back to me. That's no lunch *two* days in a row. When school was over, he was waiting with a shaken-up can of soda that he sprayed all over me. The soda bubbles ran down my shirt and into my pants, leaving a gummy trail.

"I feel really sticky," I said to Stevie as we went home together.

"Dr . . . Pepper," said Stevie. "Stickiest . . . soda . . . there . . . is . . . Sligo . . . did . . . his . . . homework."

"Well," I said, trying to find a bright side as if there was one, "if I can get through this week, Survivor Day will be easy. Reese is making lists of our strengths and weaknesses, so we have all the events covered in the best way."

Reese was doing more work for Survivor Day than he had done all his years in school. I had to admit it was good having somebody like that on your team. But don't tell Reese I said that.

Stevie's wheels slowed down, and he looked at me. "And . . . your . . . biggest . . . weakness . . . is . . . me?"

I stared down at him. What was he talking about? Then I got it. Stevie was worried that Reese didn't want to be on a team with somebody in a wheelchair. Stevie didn't know Reese very well.

"Are you kidding?" I said. "Reese thinks *I'm* the biggest weakness on the team. He says I think too much, and it makes me choke under pressure."

"You . . . do . . . think . . . too . . . much," Stevie said with a smile.

"I know that!" I said. "Have you ever tried to not think about thinking too much? It's impossible."

"So . . . Reese . . . is . . . cool . . . with . . . me?"

"He checked out your chess club records. He says you have a killer instinct and he likes that. You just have to do it sitting down."

Stevie smiled. It wasn't often people noticed his killer instinct.

When I got home, I found Reese in the kitchen icing his knuckles. They did look a little swollen. Reese pointed to each one and told me who he'd pounded with it.

"Nathan Pillsbury called me Clar-Reese," he said, pointing to the first one. "Noah Driscoll brought me a get well teddy bear with hearts on it. This one told me to try out for field hockey. Tiffany Wigglesworth offered to punish the little girl the next time she baby-sat, so I stapled her hair to the bulletin board."

Reese had had a productive day. Like I said, nobody laughs at him for long. The weird thing is, he didn't look happy. He was looking down at his ice pack and chewing on his lip.

"Why don't I feel better?" he asked me. "I kicked so much butt today. I should feel great. How come I don't?"

I couldn't believe it. Reese was practically begging me to take a shot at him, but I couldn't do it. It's like Mom says. We can call each other whatever we want, but that's because we're family. If an outsider does it, they'd better watch out.

"Okay, Reese, this is why you feel bad," I explained. "You know if *you'd* have been watching that football game, *you* would have laughed at you. Now you've made other people stop laughing, but you know it's still funny. Only it's not funny because it's you."

Reese stared at me for a long time. "Dude, is this how you go through your life, thinking about everything until it makes no sense at all?"

"Pretty much, yeah," I said.

"I'm so glad I'm normal," said Reese.

That's the last time I try to make him feel better.

"Here's what I think the problem is," Reese said. "It's that monkey. It's psyching me out. Too many bad associations."

In my mind I saw Banana Joe staring at me when I woke up this morning. We only bought the thing to get back at Dewey and that wasn't happening. Reese was freaked out, I was freaked out, and Dewey was . . .

"*Day-o!*" I heard. What was that? "*Daaaaay-o!*"

Me and Reese stared at each other. Dewey was singing in our bedroom. We started down the hallway as Dewey continued to sing.

"Six foot, seven foot, eight foot *bunch!*" Then Dewey chanted the line about daylight and wanting to go home.

"It's 'The Banana Boat Song,'" Reese said.

"And I'll bet I know who he's singing it for."

Sure enough, when we got into the room, Dewey was dancing around in front of Banana Joe, who was leering more than usual. He'd lined up three rows of blue M&M's and glued them to a piece of paper at Joe's feet. Dewey was wearing a big straw hat and no shirt and the pants from his pirate costume. He had a banana in each hand and was shaking them while he danced and yelled out the words to the song.

Reese and I jumped in and wrestled him to the ground. "You're gonna wanna go home, all right," Reese threatened.

"'Time to tally *me* banana, Dewey," I added. It is a great song. We love singing it — *on car trips.*

"Let me go!" Dewey wailed. "Joe wants to hear the song."

Reese grabbed Dewey's bananas and held one of them up to his throat. "Listen to me, monkey boy," he growled in his enforcer voice. "Joe can't hear anything. His head is filled with sawdust."

"Yeah, he's a stuffed monkey," I said. "He can't eat M&M's, he can't be your friend, and he definitely can't bring bad luck."

"He can too!" cried Dewey.

"Dewey," I said. "Banana Joe can't do anything. Say it!"

Dewey shut his mouth and shook his head back and forth. Reese started tapping Dewey on the head with the second banana, still holding the first one under his chin. "Dewey, you know I know karate," he warned. "In the hands of a karate master, a banana is a lethal weapon." Tap, tap, tap went the banana.

"Reese, no." I played good brother. "Not the banana. Anything but that. It's inhuman."

I saw Dewey's eyes grow wide as they followed the "deadly" fruit in Reese's hand.

"Say it, Dewey," said Reese. "Say it, and it will all be over."

"Okay!" Dewey yelled. I grabbed his fingers and uncrossed them. You have to watch Dewey that way. "Banana Joe can't do anything!"

Reese stood up and peeled the banana and tossed the other one to me. We went back into the kitchen, leaving Dewey sitting on the floor in his straw hat.

"We had to do it," I said, biting into my banana. "It was for his own good."

"And it was fun, too," Reese pointed out, eating his banana. "Now I feel better."

We smiled at each other. Then we heard Dewey again.

"I'm sooooorrrryyy!" he wailed.

"Uh-oh," I said.

We ran back into the bedroom. Dewey was standing in front of Banana Joe in the weirdest position I'd ever seen. One hand was on his opposite shoulder, and the other one was on his knee. His knees were locked together, and his nose was touching one shoulder. He looked like he was playing some strange game of Twister with himself.

"Dewey, what are you doing?" I asked.

He just looked at me helplessly. Reese and I went over and tried to straighten him up.

No luck. He was glued that way. The bottle of glue lay on the floor in front of Banana Joe.

CHAPTER EIGHT

"**O**w!" yelped Dewey as Mom bumped his shoulder the next morning at breakfast. She'd hit the spot where his hand had been glued the day before. When Mom had come home from work and found Dewey glued, she'd interrogated me and Reese. When she was satisfied we hadn't done it, she grabbed both of Dewey's hands and yanked them free. Dewey got unstuck, but it was pretty painful.

"It's the best way to do it," Mom explained. "It's like a Band-Aid. Rip it off quickly. Who wants dinner?"

Dewey hadn't said much about Joe since the banana incident, but I caught him looking at the monkey a lot. I didn't touch Banana Joe at all last night, but when I went to sleep, he was facing Dewey, and when I woke up, he was facing Reese. I don't even want to think about it.

Reese and I had had enough. We'd come to a decision. We were going to throw the hominid (that's Banana Joe) out right after breakfast. Dewey said Banana Joe would come back to get us, but we told him that was totally stupid.

"Malcolm, I want you to start mental conditioning," Reese said at breakfast.

"What?"

"It's a karate thing. It will help get rid of your monkey mind," Reese said, trying to sound like a karate master. "That way, when you're under pressure, you'll have the eye of the tiger."

"Whatever," I said.

I couldn't wait to see what the eye of the tiger was like.

"You're going to need the strength of the ox," Sensei Reese continued, "the swiftness of the rabbit and . . ."

"The cunning of the chipmunk?" I suggested. Reese looked at me in disgust.

"Don't mock me, grasshopper," said Reese. He loves *Kung Fu: The Legend Continues*. "On Survivor Day, you'll need my wisdom to triumph."

"I want to triumph on Survivor Day," Dewey said. "I want to triumph! I want to triumph! I want to triumph!"

"You want to shut up," barked Reese.

"I want to eat breakfast," I said, reaching for the orange juice.

"Mom!" Dewey whined.

"Stop picking on Dewey," Mom said. "You're his big brothers. You're supposed to protect him and help him, not make his life a living nightmare."

Mom didn't know much about being a big brother. That's *exactly* what you're supposed to do.

After breakfast, all three of us went back to our room to get Banana Joe. For a minute we all just stared at him. We tried to act like we just came back to get our books, but I swear he was on to us. Finally, Reese grabbed the monkey, shoved him into his backpack, and zipped it over Joe's head.

"Let's go," said Reese.

Dewey stayed behind me, so I was between him and the monkey.

"Bye, Mom!" Reese said a little too cheerfully.

"She's totally going to know something's up," I warned him.

"Why should she care?" Reese asked. "It's not her monkey."

When we got outside, we paused at the garbage can. I lifted the lid, and Reese unzipped his backpack. Dewey bit his fingernails.

"So long, Joe," Reese said, scooping him out of the bag and putting him into the trash.

I tried to put the lid on as fast as possible. I wasn't fast enough. I got a glimpse of Joe's eyes glittering up at me. I was totally relieved to get rid of him. I felt like this big weight was off my shoulders. The ape was out of my life.

We practically had to drag Dewey down the block. He kept looking back at the trash can like he was expecting Banana Joe to crawl back out of it or something.

I was smiling, thinking about Banana Joe safely in

the trash, as I got to school. Then I felt two hands on my shoulders. I dropped my knapsack as Sligo lifted me off my feet.

"Put me down!" I started to yell, but it was too late. Sligo dumped me in the big metal trash can on the side of the playground.

"Hey, look," Sligo said, grinning down at me. "Canned Malcolm!"

His buddies started laughing as if he'd said something funny. I was almost grateful when he slammed the lid down so I couldn't hear them. I sat there in the dark until the bullies walked away, thinking of how weird this was. This is what I'd just done to Banana Joe. Could that mean something?

I was still thinking about that when the lid opened slowly. "Malcolm?" a girl's voice said.

It was Julie Houlerman! Of all the people in the world, she was the *last* one I would want to find me in a garbage can.

"Are you all right?" she asked in a really nice way.

I tried to smile. "Sure," I said. Yeah, like I always sit in the garbage can before school. Doesn't everyone?

Julie reached in to help me out. I took her hand. It was kind of like we were holding hands for a second. It's no big deal. It's just something I noticed. I hauled myself out of the can, really glad it hadn't been totally filled with garbage.

"Hi," I said. What do you say to the girl who just found you in a garbage can?

"Sligo shouldn't pick on kids smaller than he is," Julie pointed out.

Great, she thinks I'm a shrimp.

"Oh, I could take him," I lied. "He just caught me by surprise."

Julie smiled like the way Mom smiled when Dewey told her he'd just killed a bear in the bathtub.

"This is the worst week of my life." Wait, did I say that out loud?

"What's wrong, Malcolm?" asked Julie. "Is it your family again?"

"Actually, it's a monkey," I replied. I couldn't believe it, but I started telling her the whole story of Banana Joe. It was like I was listening to myself? Telling myself to shut up? But I still kept talking. When I was finished, Julie looked concerned.

"Gee, Malcolm," she said. "I've never met anyone cursed before."

So is that a good thing or a bad thing?

"Well, I got rid of the beast this morning," I said. "So I'm not cursed anymore."

"Are you sure?" she asked. "Don't you usually have to do something, like, special to get rid of the bad luck?"

"I didn't do anything special," I admitted. "I just put it in the garbage can."

Julie's eyebrows went up and her eyes, which are a really nice shade of blue, darted over to the garbage can I just came out of.

"I know how this looks," I said. "But I'm sure it's just

a coincidence. I'll never see Banana Joe again. He's landfill."

Julie still looked worried, but she smiled politely. "I'm sure you're right, Malcolm."

I smiled back just as the bell rang.

"I guess I'll see you around," I said.

Julie nodded. I turned and started to walk to the trailer. Maybe my luck was starting to change after all. Julie and I managed a whole conversation where I didn't end up looking like an idiot. You know, once I climbed out of the garbage can? I think I was pretty cool.

I felt a tap on my shoulder and turned around. It was Julie. "What's up?" I asked casually.

"You have a banana peel stuck to your butt," Julie said gently. "I thought you should know."

As Julie spoke, the peel on my butt came unstuck and plopped down to the ground behind me.

"Thanks," I said weakly. "I think it's gone now."

I managed to avoid Sligo by volunteering to exercise the frogs during lunch and running straight home after school. Maybe it just took a while for the curse to lift. *It had to be gone by now*, I thought as I closed the door behind me and walked into the kitchen. I took out one of Dad's bologna Oreos and was just about to take a bite when I heard a scream from my bedroom.

I ran down the hall. "What is it?" I asked, coming into the room.

I was just in time to see Dewey's feet disappear under the bed where he was hiding. Reese was standing with his mouth open, not moving.

Finally, he managed to lift a finger and point to the dresser.

Banana Joe sat grinning at all of us.

Sometimes they come back. You think you've gotten rid of something, you put it in the trash can, and then you come home from school and it's in your bedroom waiting for you.

Okay, so we've got a beast in an organ grinder's cap in our room. What do we do now? Dewey swears he didn't have anything to do with Banana Joe's return, and I believe him because he hasn't come out from under the bed for hours. Reese says he didn't do it, and he must be telling the truth because he's a terrible liar. Besides, there's no way he could fake those beads of sweat on his upper lip. Nobody else knew we'd thrown the thing out.

Somehow Banana Joe got from the garbage can back into our bedroom. Nobody knows how.

CHAPTER NINE

None of us was crazy enough to let Banana Joe stay on the dresser after that. We stuffed him back into the knapsack and put him in the closet right next to my knapsack for Survivor Day. On the outside both knapsacks looked the same. They were red with an extra pocket on the outside. You couldn't tell that one of them had a cursed beast inside. I put a Chiquita sticker from one of Dewey's bananas on the one with Banana Joe so I would know. He didn't come out of the closet Wednesday or Thursday night. I know that because I sat awake both nights. It turns out that in one night, the streetlight on the corner of our street flickers 248 times. I counted. If I got a quarter for every time it would flicker, I would make sixty-two dollars a night. I'd only have to stay up five nights in a row to make three hundred and ten dollars. That's enough money for a one-way ticket for Banana Joe to fly far away from here.

"You . . . look . . . terrible," Stevie told me as I walked and he rolled home from school on Friday afternoon.

"You would, too, if you had psycho-monkey in your closet," I grumbled.

Stevie shook his head. "I ... told ... you ... There's ... only ... one ... way ..." Stevie began.

"Sacred ground," I cut in. "I know." Okay, I know it sounds like a crazy idea? But after not sleeping for fifty-six hours and twenty-three minutes, I figured why not? "What do I have to do?"

Stevie smiled. He was loving this. I would have killed him if I wasn't so tired.

"You're ... going ... to ... need ... some ... special ... items."

According to Stevie, in order to do an official curse removal, we had to perform a ceremony that involved dead bugs, human hair, and a special rattle that Stevie happened to own. I thought I could cover the rest. Dewey had been collecting dead bugs for years, and we always had hair around the house from the day once a month when my mom shaved my dad's body hair. Don't ask.

"Okay," I said. "You swear that if I can get this stuff you can perform a ceremony that will get rid of Banana Joe forever?"

"If ... you ... can ... get ... me ... out ... of ... my ... house," said Stevie. "I ... can ... get ... rid ... of ... Banana ... Joe."

Getting Stevie out of his house wasn't going to be easy. His parents are a little overprotective. They put him to bed at eight o'clock. And they have sensors in his bedroom so if he moves after that, an alarm goes off.

"I'll come by tonight," I promised. "With Banana Joe."

When I got home, I realized I didn't know where we were supposed to find sacred ground. My dad considers the stock car racetrack the most sacred ground he knows. Reese would say it was the arcade at the mall where he beat the high score on Mortal Kombat. For a while Dewey was really into the space behind the hamper in the bathroom, but I don't think those places are what Stevie means by sacred ground. If I was going to find the right place for Banana Joe, I was going to have to ask an expert. *That's* my brother Francis.

Francis would never be scared of a stuffed monkey. If he were my partner for Survivor Day, we'd win no problem. Francis always wins. Before he got sent to military school? Somebody bet Francis that he couldn't get out of school for a week without getting into trouble. Francis started a flesh-eating virus scare, and everybody got out of school for a week. It was so cool. He won the bet and got a shark tooth necklace that's really excellent.

Francis was sure to know where I could find sacred ground. I called him as soon as I took my jacket off.

"Young master Malcolm!" Francis said when he got on the phone. "Please tell me you're calling to say Mom and Dad want me to come home."

"I wish." Everything would be better if Francis were here. "I called to ask you something. You know Survivor Day is coming up tomorrow?"

"Absolutely," Francis said. "Sorry I can't be there. I

sent you something for good luck. Tell Reese I said not to kill you."

"I will. But I need to know something. If you were me and you needed to find sacred ground, where would you go?"

Francis didn't even have to think. "The cemetery next to the church," he replied. "If you need to get into it after dark, cut through the yard of the redbrick house on Grove Street. There's a section of the fence that I cut so that you don't have to climb over it."

"Thanks!" I said. I knew Francis would know.

"What do you need sacred ground for?" Francis asked.

I explained that we had accidentally bought this cursed monkey that we couldn't get rid of. I told him all the things that had been going on. I wasn't worried about sounding like a kid to Francis anymore. Now I knew we were dealing with an evil entity destroying the lives of everything in its path. Francis would respect that.

"I see your problem," Francis said when I was finished. "You said this girl Julie found you in the garbage can. Was there anything wet or rotten in the can with you?"

I thought about it. "No," I said. "Mostly it was candy wrappers."

I heard Francis breathe a sigh of relief.

"You're okay," he said. "You can recover from that. When are you getting rid of the monkey?"

"Tonight," I said. "I hope."

"Good luck," said Francis. "May the force be with you."

Then I heard a door slam on Francis's end, and someone yelled, "Cadet, I want to see you in my office on the double!"

It sounded like Francis was in trouble.

"I was framed," Francis whispered into the phone. "Tell Mom it wasn't my fault." Then the line went dead. Francis never gets a break.

I found Reese and Dewey watching TV in the living room, as far away from Banana Joe as possible.

"Okay," I announced. "I found out how to get rid of Banana Joe." I explained Stevie's instructions to Reese.

"I'm in," said Reese. "That monkey's outta here."

"Banana Joe is not nice," said Dewey with a shiver.

I gave Reese the lowdown on Stevie's high-security house. We had to find a way to get Stevie outside without his parents knowing. I knew Reese would think it was a challenge.

"I'll need my suction-tipped grappling hook," Reese said, already planning the break-in. "With the steel-woven flexi-cord. When we get to Stevie's house I'll . . . Wait," he said, looking at me. "How are we going to get out of our house?"

Uh-oh, I thought. He's right. Stevie's house might have high-tech sensors that go off if you touch the floor, but we had a more deadly and sophisticated surveillance system. We had Mom.

"What are we going to do?" asked Reese.

I thought about it. "To sneak out of the house, we're going to need a distraction."

"Where do we get one of those?" asked Reese.

I glanced over at Dewey, who was hitting himself on the head with a spoon and singing "I'm a Little Teapot."

"I think we found our distraction," I said.

Dewey agreed that after dinner he would get Mom and Dad's attention . . . IF we let him be on our team for Survivor Day. "That's blackmail!" I said. But Dewey wouldn't budge. It was totally unfair. Odds are that Dewey would have done something to get Mom and Dad's attention anyway, but we couldn't take that chance. "You're in," I told Dewey reluctantly.

"You win. This time," Reese muttered. "But mess up, and you're going with Banana Joe."

That night we had extra-cheese macaroni and cheese for dinner because Reese said it was good for endurance. I don't know what he's talking about, but I like macaroni and cheese, so I didn't complain.

"I've got some eggs," my dad said. "You boys can eat two raw before bed tonight. That's what I always did when I was in training for the skating championships."

"Cool," said Reese.

"I don't think so," I said. Was my dad serious? Who eats raw eggs?

"I'm training for Survivor Day, too," said Dewey

with a smile a mile wide. He was really rubbing it in.

Mom's eyebrows went up, and she looked at me and Reese. We shrugged.

"When did that happen?" Mom asked. She sounded happy, but really suspicious, that we were letting Dewey on the team.

"This afternoon," I said.

Mom stared us down with her truth-seeking laser eyes. "Why?" she asked.

I stared at my macaroni. "Because he's our brother and we love him," I lied.

Reese gave Mom what he thought was a convincing brotherly smile and put his arm around Dewey. Nothing less than an evil beast would have gotten Reese to put his arm around Dewey. We were really working together, even if this probably wasn't what Mom had in mind.

Dewey grinned and then he gave Reese a big kiss on the cheek. Oh, man, and I thought I was having bad luck this week. I'd rather have my sandwich licked again by Sligo. Reese kept control of himself — barely. Then he said he had to go to the bathroom.

While Reese was washing his face twenty times, I opened the closet door and grabbed the knapsack with the Chiquita sticker on it — the one with Banana Joe in it. Reese came out of the bathroom. "Are we good to go?" he asked. He was dressed in black from head to toe with his grappling hook hanging from his belt.

I listened for Dewey in the other room. "Give him a minute."

From the living room, I heard the opening bars of "The Banana Boat Song" blasting out of the CD player. *"Day-o! Daaay-o!"*

Reese and I tiptoed into the hallway and looked into the living room. Dewey was dressed in the straw hat and pirate pants again, bananas in both hands. Mom and Dad were on the couch clapping along. Reese was pushing to get to the door. "Let's go," he whispered.

"Wait for it," I said.

In the next second, we got what we were waiting for. Mom and Dad singing at the top of their lungs. "Daylight come and me wanna go home!" We knew they couldn't resist "The Banana Boat Song."

Reese and I slipped down the hallway past the living room where Mom and Dad and Dewey had formed a conga line with Dewey shaking the bananas at the front.

"Phase One complete," Reese said as we shut the front door behind us.

CHAPTER TEN

When we got to Stevie's house, the lights in his room were off, which meant he was probably already sent to bed. Reese insisted we secure the perimeter by walking all the way around the house and looking in all the windows. There wasn't much going on. Stevie's parents were in the kitchen. We watched them for a minute. They seemed to be sharpening pencils and then scribbling with them until the points weren't sharp anymore. Stevie isn't allowed to handle sharp objects. Reese shook his head in amazement. "They have a car, a satellite dish, and no bedtime," he said sadly. "And this is what they do with their time."

We continued on around the house until we got to Stevie's bedroom window, which was half open. I made a noise like a cat — that was our signal. In a second, I heard Stevie's answering pigeon call.

"Okay," I told Reese, "do your stuff."

Reese grinned. He stuck his head through the window. Stevie was sitting up in his bed, fully dressed. Next to him on the bed he'd arranged a pillow and blanket to look like him in case his parents came to check on him. He waved at us. I reached in and pulled out the bag he'd placed by the window with all his curse busting equipment in it. It smelled like sawdust and pepper.

Reese swung his grappling hook like a lasso and tossed it toward the doorknob of Stevie's room. I can't believe it, but he actually got it on the first try. Even Reese looked surprised . . . and disappointed that nobody but me was there to see it.

Reese handed me the other end of the flexi-cord. "Don't drop it," he warned me. "Make sure it's tight."

I held onto the rope and Reese pulled himself over the windowsill. He hung upside down on the cord and pulled himself hand over hand toward the door to Stevie's room with his feet hooked over the cord so they didn't touch the ground. When he got to the door, he looked to Stevie.

"Over . . . there," Stevie whispered, pointing to the a little red button on the wall next to the door.

Reese reached out and pressed the button, turning off the sensor.

"Yesssss!" Stevie whispered.

Okay, Reese did have the skills. I had to admit it.

Reese quickly rolled up the cord and hung it on his belt. He pushed Stevie's wheelchair over to the window and, folding it flat, handed it over the sill to me. Stevie wrapped his arms around Reese's shoulders. Just as Reese was about to pick him up, we heard Stevie's parents coming down the hall.

"Incoming!" Reese hissed.

Reese dropped Stevie back onto his bed and dove

73

under the covers beside him. Only the tips of his hair were sticking out when Stevie's parents opened the door.

"Hey, Champ," Stevie's dad whispered. He was wearing a fuzzy sweater and a bow tie.

Stevie kept his eyes closed and smiled like he was having a nice dream.

"He's like a little angel," his mother sighed.

I wondered if they'd change their minds about that if they knew what else was under the covers. Stevie's parents blew him a kiss and backed out of the doorway, shutting the door behind them. Reese sat up beside Stevie and glared at both of us one after the other.

"This didn't happen," he said, crawling out from under the covers.

It was a shame I could never tell anybody about this. Well, maybe Francis.

Reese picked Stevie up again and took him to the window. Reese and I lowered him out feet first into the chair, and Reese crawled out after him.

"Phase Two, complete," said Reese.

"Let's . . . roll," said Stevie.

We jogged to the cemetery with Reese pushing Stevie and me running alongside with the bag of equipment and the backpack. We turned down Grove Street, and I looked for the redbrick house.

"There it is," I whispered. "The lights are on, so we have to keep quiet."

We rolled Stevie over the grass toward the chain-link fence that separated the backyard from the cemetery next door.

"Where's the hole?" Reese whispered, looking at the fence.

I checked the whole fence carefully. Francis would never make a hole that somebody might see and fix. I hoped it was big enough to get Stevie through. Finally, I found it. "Over here," I called softly, pulling back a section of the fence like a big door. It was wide enough for all of us to get through. Francis is so cool.

I closed the fence behind us, and we walked into the cemetery. In the corner where we had just come through, there was a big tree and at the bottom of it there was all this stuff: teddy bears, flowers, and lots of notes. I picked one up and read it. It said, "Dear Francis, I'll never forget our date at the Taco Shack. Stay away from the hot sauce. Love, Patti. XOXOXO."

I couldn't believe all this stuff was for Francis. And it was all from girls. See? Everybody wanted Francis to come home. It was like sacred ground in the sacred ground.

"I'm burying it here," said Reese, taking a shovel out of Stevie's bag and starting to dig. "Next to Debbie Kinderman's clay statue of Francis."

"No!" I said. "We're not putting Banana Joe with Francis's stuff. Then he'll have bad luck and he doesn't need any more. Besides, we're too close to the fence here. The monkey might tunnel his way out or something."

"Tunnel . . . his . . . way . . . out?" Stevie said, giving me a funny look.

"You are so whacked," laughed Reese. "He can't tunnel out. He's zipped in a backpack."

"He got out of the trash can," I reminded him.

"The trash can didn't have a zipper," Reese said, like it was obvious.

"What's that supposed to mean?" I demanded. Out of the corner of my eye I could see Stevie watching us, like we were the funniest thing he'd ever seen. I didn't see what was so funny about having a brother who was a complete idiot.

"How is he supposed to open the zipper from the inside?" Reese said.

Stevie grinned. "Even . . . Houdini . . . couldn't . . . do . . . that," he said.

"He could use a magnet," I suggested. "He could stick his hooked claw through the zipper teeth, he could chew through the nylon from the inside out. There's a hundred ways a hairy fiend could get out of a knapsack. Use your brain!"

I wasn't going to argue about this anymore. I grabbed the knapsack and started running down a row of tombstones. Reese was after me in a second. He jumped me from behind, and I dropped the knapsack. We were on a hill so we rolled down over each other. First Reese was on top of me, then I was on top of Reese. We kept trying to hit each other no matter which way we were facing.

Above us, Stevie had picked up the knapsack and was rolling down after us. He was calling something. It sounded like, "Look . . . out."

I gave Reese a big push, and he fell off me, but we both kept rolling. Suddenly, it was like there was no ground to roll on, like I was rolling over a cliff. I grabbed on to the edge with my hands and stopped myself just before I fell into a big hole that was totally going to be somebody's grave. Reese was next to me, looking into the same hole.

"Dude," he said. "Can we just drop the knapsack in here?"

That would be cool. The hole was already dug.

Stevie rolled to a stop next to us. "Can't . . . bury . . . him . . . here," he said. "They'd . . . see . . . him . . . at . . . the . . . funeral."

Stevie had a point. Somebody would be bound to notice a bright red knapsack with a dead monkey in an open grave.

Stevie pointed to a good spot. "Put . . . him . . . there," he said.

Reese would never listen to me, but he didn't mind listening to Stevie. We started digging.

"Do . . . you . . . guys . . . fight . . . like . . . this . . . every . . . day?" Stevie asked.

Reese shrugged. "Yes." He dropped a pile of dirt on my shoe on purpose.

"On average about forty-two hours and eighteen

minutes a week," I said, tossing my shovelful of dirt at Reese. "Unless we're grounded. Then we fight more."

"Awesome," said Stevie.

The weird thing is, he really meant it. I guess when you're used to pencil sharpening parents, two brothers who were always ready to kill each other would be an improvement. I had to admit that my house was never boring.

Reese and I finally got the hole dug. Reese dumped his last shovelful over my head. Then he dumped another shovelful on Stevie's lap, which made Stevie kind of happy.

"There you go, Wheels," Reese said.

When Reese turned around, Stevie grabbed the waistband of his underwear and gave Reese a wedgie. It was like he was family. Burying a hexed hominid with someone is a real bonding experience.

I handed the knapsack to Reese and he gave it to Stevie. Stevie held it above the hole we'd dug. "Hasta...la...vista...Banana...beast," said Stevie, dropping the knapsack. It made a scary thump when it hit the ground. For a second, I didn't move. I swear I thought the monkey was going leap out of the hole right at my face. Then me and Reese started shoveling as fast as we could. I think we were both imagining Joe digging his way out as fast as we could bury him.

Finally, the knapsack was completely covered with

dirt. Stevie reached into the bag and pulled out this weird hat with feathers and snakeskins and beads hanging from it. When he put it on, he looked like a combination Indian chief, witch doctor, and science club president. Stevie shook his rattle and howled.

"Is this what you study in your genius class?" Reese asked as Stevie sprinkled salt on the ground and told us to scatter the dead bugs and my dad's hair around in a circle.

"We're allowed to study whatever we want as long as it has educational value."

Stevie started chanting. "Oooh . . . eeeh . . . oooh . . . ah! . . . ah! . . . ting! . . . tang! . . . walla! . . . walla! . . . bing! . . . bang!" he sang.

I turned back to Reese, who looked confused. "Sometimes the educational value is not visible to the naked eye," I admitted. Stevie was turning his wheelchair in circles and wailing like a siren.

"Whatever," said Reese. Who was *he* to say what had educational value?

Reese and I kept scattering the bugs and the hair. We got kind of into it and it was fun.

You know, if you ever have a chance to be in a curse removal ceremony yourself? You should definitely do it. Mom never let us throw Dad's hair around the house, and I have to tell you, it was really cool.

When we'd danced around the circle three times chanting, "Walla-walla bing-bang!" Stevie raised his rattle and shook it hard.

"That . . . did . . . it," said Stevie.

Reese and I grinned. Suddenly, I realized we were in a cemetery at night with dead bugs and Stevie in a weird hat. This was so cool! I wish Francis could see me. This is why it stinks that he's in military school.

Reese crossed his arms over his chest and nodded. "Phase Three. Complete."

The monkey that would not die was gone. I could feel it. The shadow of supernatural horror had lifted.

I think when I'm old, like maybe thirty, I'll remember this as one of the best moments in my life.

Suddenly, we heard a dog bark behind us. There was a man with a flashlight walking beside it. "Hey you, kids!" the man shouted. "No trespassing!"

Okay, so maybe it was the best thirty seconds of my life. As the guy let his dog off the leash, me and Reese started running, pushing Stevie in front of us. The teeth on that dog looked even sharper than Banana Joe's. We skidded past the teddy bears girls had left for Frances and I pulled open the fence for Reese and Stevie. I'd just closed it as the dog ran up and jumped. For a second I thought he was going to make it over, but he didn't. See? My good luck was starting already.

It was a lot easier getting Stevie back into his room than it was getting him out. When we got to his house, his parents were spraying for dust mites. They had gas masks on that made it hard to hear anything. How Stevie could be related to these people was beyond me.

"See you tomorrow, Wheels," Reese said as he climbed out Stevie's window. "We meet again at 0800 hours."

"Roger," said Stevie, waving to me.

Reese and I walked home together to our now finally monkey-free home.

*E*verything seemed better with that monkey off my back. Reese and I didn't fight at all before we went to bed. I wasn't even mad about having Dewey on the team tomorrow.

Without Banana Joe, I felt like we had a real shot at being Last of the Mohicans. I'd already survived Banana Joe, Doug Sligo, and a cemetery dog. Nothing at Survivor Day could be as hard to survive.

CHAPTER ELEVEN

The next morning, Saturday, at breakfast, Mom found a package on our doorstep. She brought it into the kitchen where me, Reese, Dewey, and Dad were eating special macro-balanced waffles that would optimize connective tissue function. Reese found the recipe in *Man's Man* magazine. Dad called it the Breakfast of Champions.

"Malcolm, somebody sent you something," Mom said, putting the package on the table. It was from Francis!

"He said he was sending me something for good luck." I ripped it open. I reached in and pulled out something on a string. I couldn't believe it. Francis had sent me his shark's tooth.

"Wasn't that nice of your brother," said Mom. "Sending you an old tooth."

"Excellent," I said, turning the shark tooth over in my hands.

"Remember the way of the shark," said Sensei Reese. "You stop swimming, you die. That means no thinking. Just swim."

I put the shark tooth around my neck.

"There was this kid in my class," piped up Dewey. "He had a shark. He brought it to school, and the shark ate all the chocolate pudding."

"It did not," said Reese.

Dewey didn't care. Why should he? He was going to Survivor Day.

When we got to the park for Survivor Day, kids and parents were all hanging around near the edge of Crystal Lake, where we were going to be racing in canoes. The canoe race was worth more points than all the other contests. I saw Stevie with his parents and we went over to them.

"Hey . . . Malcolm," said Stevie. It was almost hard to tell it was him, because he was covered in so much protective padding.

Stevie's mom and dad stood behind him and smiled proudly. "Stevie's dad was state Boggle champion three years in a row," Stevie's mom said.

I didn't even know we had a state Boggle champion.

Stevie's dad nodded. "Champion," he said. "Champ, pin, ham, pan, in, ion, map, chip, camp, mop, campion, campo, him, can, hip, nip, cap, pion, pom, hop, pima."

My dad smiled. "Great," he said.

"Stevie's so excited about this competition," his mom said. "He made sure to get extra sleep last night."

Stevie smiled secretly at me and I smiled back.

Reese came over with a piece of paper. "Okay, I got a list of the events we're signed up for and I figured out which one of us should do each one." There were a lot of events and a lot of teams. The only contest everyone was in together was the final canoe race.

"The first thing we're in is the Battering Ram," Reese said. "That's where you put on a helmet and have to defend yourself against attack with just your head."

"That sounds like you," I said. "I use my head for other things."

"Exactly," Reese agreed. "Next is the Wall of Fear. We choose one team member to put on a Velcro suit and get thrown at the targets on a sticky wall."

"Dewey," we all said. We'd been training for this our whole life.

"Then comes the Highway of Doom. It's an obstacle course for racing cars. Wheels, that's you."

Stevie nodded.

"Next up is the Race of Death through the woods. Malcolm, do you think you can run without thinking about it?"

I tugged on my shark tooth. "I think so. I mean, I guess. I think . . ."

Reese shook his head in disgust.

"The next one is something called the Muscles of Stone. It's a test of endurance. We all do that one. Then there's the canoe race. That's where we crush them."

Mom gave each of us a big hug, including Stevie. "Just do your best," she said. "Now get 'em."

Dad saluted us with the special sign of the Brotherhood of the Wheel. That's what Dad called competitive skaters like himself. "You're all warriors," he said. "It's in your blood."

"Yours, too, son," Stevie's dad said. "You come from a long line of gladiators. Gladiator, glad, rot, data, lad, lit, tag, rig, iota, lid, rid, rat, lag, tor, toril, aid, laid, lair, raid, dial."

Reese, Dewey, and I backed Stevie slowly away from his dad and his weird word game.

The Battering Ram contest was a real no-brainer. Reese was killing the competition. Reese butted everything his helmet came near: soccer balls, other players, their moms, a judge. When all the judges had ducked under the table for protection, they blew the whistle and declared Reese the winner. We won the first event. It was so cool.

And it totally meant our bad luck was over — no Banana Joe, we were good to go!

I was watching Reese take off his helmet when something really cold slid down my back. I turned around to see Sligo and his team grinning at me. I shook out the ice cube that Sligo had just put down my shirt.

"Your team's going down," leered Sligo.

Another team walked by, led by Martin Stephens from my class. They were discussing their strategy for the Sticky Wall. Sligo grabbed Martin and dumped the rest of his Coke over his head.

"Now you'll be extra sticky," Sligo sneered.

Martin glared at him. "You have serious behavior issues," he snapped. "Get some help."

Dewey was all suited up in Velcro and just itching to get on the wall. We were all lined up and ready to throw. I took a look at Sligo's team. Besides Sligo himself, there were two kids built like Mack trucks and one really really tall kid. They were throwing one of the short ones at the wall, but their aim wasn't very good. They kept missing the target.

Dewey, on the other hand, just hit a bull's-eye every time. "We have got to get one of these at home," Reese said as we hurled Dewey through the air and he landed with a smack flat on the wall.

That was when Sligo pulled something sneaky. He took a container of baby powder out of his pocket. He pretended he was congratulating people, but he was really shaking it over everybody's Velcro suit except the guy on his team. Now nobody was sticking to the wall. Kids would just slide off and fall on the ground.

Except Dewey. Dewey was born sticky. Usually it's just gross. It's never been a plus before. Today it was the greatest. Reese and I just kept tossing him, and he kept landing with a big smile. "Do it again! Do it again!" he called. We peeled Dewey off the wall and all gave him a high five. Boy, was Sligo mad when we won that event, too.

After the Wall of Fear, we got Stevie into his car for the obstacle race. All the controls were hand-operated. It was really all about steering.

"Okay, Wheels," Reese instructed. "See the path, follow the path. Be one with the car."

Stevie studied the course. "Just . . . like . . . the . . . cafeteria . . . when . . . the . . . bell . . . rings," he said. "Obstacles . . . everywhere . . . it's . . . all . . . in . . . the . . . steering."

I held Stevie's wheelchair for him. My dad gave him the Brotherhood of the Wheel salute. Stevie's parents looked scared to death.

Sligo was driving the car right next to Stevie.

"Gentlemen, start your engines," said a teacher waving a checkered flag.

Sligo turned to Stevie. "Crash and burn, Krel-boyne," Sligo spit.

Stevie didn't even look at him. "Eat . . . my . . . dust."

And they're off! Stevie zigzagged around the rubber cones, taking the first part of the course easily, giving Sligo a major case of road rage. He started banging into other cars like it was a demolition derby, knocking them off the course. The judges just thought he was a bad driver. After a few minutes, he and Stevie were the only drivers left in the home-stretch.

Sligo drove up alongside Stevie and then turned his wheel sharply so that he banged into the side of Stevie's car. Stevie tilted up on two wheels. For a second, I was sure he was going to flip over, but he just kept driving.

"How does he do that?" Reese marveled.

"Francis did it once with Mom's car," I said. "But it was an accident."

Stevie pulled ahead of Sligo, tipping back onto all four wheels. He crossed the finish line and ran straight into the blow-up moon-walk tent. It was like a big balloon, so Stevie was fine. He pulled off his helmet and waved to his new fans. Everybody, except Stevie's mom and my parents, was cheering and clapping because it was amazing. Stevie's mom had fainted, and my mom and dad were reviving her.

So far we'd done really well in our events. Now it was my turn. What if I was the only one on our team to lose? I mean, it was okay if Stevie lost because *he* didn't have to live with Reese. Reese was *expecting* Dewey to lose, so he couldn't really damage his reputation. He wasn't old enough to have one. If *I* lost, I could pretty much give up on life.

"You might as well sit this one out," Sligo told me, pointing to my opponent. It was the tall kid. This kid looked like two legs with a platform and then a head on top. There was no way I could run as fast as he could.

"Looks like a tough guy to beat," somebody said behind me. It was my dad.

"It's impossible," I said.

"No, son, it's very possible," Dad said. "Look at the course you're going to run. That boy is an antelope. You're a rabbit. Antelopes command the open savannah. Rabbits rule the woods."

I looked at my dad, trying to figure out what he was trying to say. Maybe he was just trying to get my mind off my certain defeat by confusing me. I squeezed my shark's tooth and went to the starting line.

Dewey stared up at the tall guy on Sligo's team. "Are you a giant?" he asked. "Are you going to eat my brother?"

Looking at the guy next to me, I couldn't help mentally working out the leg length to stride ratio and how much faster than me that meant he could run.

Reese yelled at me from the sidelines: "Just run, don't think!"

The race started. Two kids were immediately wiped out by Sligo tripping them. Once we entered the woods, we lost two Krelboynes to allergy attacks. It was just me and the antelope. I was running along behind him, sure there was no way I could win, until something happened. We came to some trees with branches that were kind of low. Antelope boy had to brush them out of the way and duck under them. That slowed him down. A lot. I ran right under them, just like a rabbit. I couldn't believe it. My dad's story actually made sense! I started running faster. I really had a chance!

The antelope was still pretty fast, but I followed the way of the rabbit right to the finish line. Stevie was the first one to see us come out of the woods.

"Oh . . . my . . . god," he yelled. "It's . . . Malcolm!"

My whole family started chanting, "Go, rabbit, go! Go, rabbit, go!"

Normally, that would be pretty embarrassing, but

who cares? I was winning the race! I crossed the finish line an eighth of a millimeter in front of the antelope. The crowd went wild.

Reese completely lost control. He ran up to me, threw his arms around me, and picked me up. I raised my arms up in a "V" for victory. I saw my dad wipe away a tear. The shark's tooth bounced against my chest. I was ready for anything. Again, I remembered the monkey. So buried!

Then we lost the next three events. We played Capture the Glory and Dewey was right near the goal when we passed him the flag that said GLORY on it. Then he saw the giant on Sligo's team and ran back in the other direction shouting "Fe fi fo fum!" When we did the Tug of Force, Stevie forgot to set the brake on his wheelchair and rolled right over to the other side. I ran the Obstacle Course of Certain Death against Sligo, who kept dropping extra obstacles behind him. It was the Eskimo pie wrapper that did me in. Those things are slippery. I complained to the judges, but they just made a speech about littering.

We were feeling pretty down before the Muscles of Stone contest. In that one everybody had to kneel on the ground, hands clasped behind our heads. Stevie got to sit in his chair. The idea was that the last person left who hadn't moved, won. One by one, kids dropped out. Reese and I just smiled. I thought back to last weekend when we'd spent much more time than this kneeling in the hallway with our hands behind our head for dropping Dewey out of the tree. Mom had totally prepared us for this one.

"I told you it would help us win Survivor Day," Reese reminded me.

"Yeah," I said. "Too bad these other kids don't have moms who torture them regularly."

I glanced over at Mom, who was smiling proudly. Mom had trained us well.

We had a break after Muscles of Stone so that our arms wouldn't be numb for the canoe race. I thought this was a good time to get out the container of muscle-building fruit punch I'd brought. I grabbed my knapsack.

"Try . . . this," Stevie said. "Pro . . . performance . . . turbo . . . drink . . . made . . . for . . . astronauts."

I put down my knapsack. We all tried Stevie's drink. It tasted like cherry-vanilla chalk, so it had to be good for you.

As I drank it, I figured out how many points all the teams had. We were in third place behind Martin Stephen's team in first and, I couldn't believe it, *Sligo's* team in second. We still had a chance to win, but we'd have to come in first in the canoe race. It was worth triple points and it would jump us ahead of the other two teams. I took another swig of cherry-vanilla chalk and picked up my knapsack.

Me, Reese, and Dewey piled into the canoe. Dewey was wearing three pairs of water wings just in case. We paddled slowly out to the starting line. Stevie was calling something from the shore. It sounded like, "Don't ... stand ... up!"

We started off pretty well in the race. Sligo's strategy was to eliminate as much competition as possible right at the beginning by capsizing the other boats when the judges weren't looking. We could hear shouts of, "You jerk!" "Cut it out!" and "So long, suckers!" behind us as we paddled along, but so far Sligo hadn't been caught.

"Hey, Brain Boy," Reese said as he rowed. "Are we on the right course for the finish line? We should be going due east."

"I'll check it out," I said. I had a compass in my knapsack. I pulled it out from under my seat and unzipped the top. I reached in and pulled out ...

"Banana Joe!!!"

CHAPTER TWELVE

"**A**aaauuuggghhh!"

I screamed and dropped the fiend from beyond the grave in the boat. Reese turned around, and his eyes bugged out. Dewey jumped up on the seat. "He's coming to get us!" he screeched.

"Dewey, sit down, you little dipwad!" Reese shouted as the boat started to rock back and forth. "You'll tip us over!"

The boat lurched to one side, making Banana Joe fly up into the air. Reese and I jumped up to get away from the flying monkey. Anybody would, even if you know you're not supposed to stand up in a canoe. The boat rolled over and we all went headfirst into the water along with Banana Joe.

"He's got me!" Reese yelled. One of Banana Joe's claws was hooked onto his T-shirt. I batted him away — and Banana Joe sunk to the bottom of Crystal Lake.

Dewey was trying to run away, but he was in the water, so he couldn't go anywhere. His water wings held him up and he spun slowly in a circle screaming, "He's going to get us! He's going to get us!"

I treaded water and thought about all the stuff I'd

buried in the graveyard instead of Banana Joe. It wasn't my fault the knapsacks were identical. Mom bought them on sale. But I knew I put the Chiquita sticker on the right one . . .

Sligo and his team appeared, laughing at us. I knew he didn't care about being Last of the Mohicans. This was what it was all about for Sligo.

"Hey, morons," Sligo yelled. "Thanks for being such losers!"

Reese swam over to Sligo. Sligo tried to poke him with his paddle, which was exactly what Reese wanted. He grabbed the end of it and with a quick jerk pulled Sligo into the water with him. The rest of Sligo's team leaned over the side of their canoe, trying to give him a hand up. So it wasn't hard for me to swim up to the side and pull the whole canoe over with them in it. Now we were all in the water.

"You are all going to die!" Sligo yelled, spitting water out of his mouth. Reese dunked Sligo from behind. I jumped on one of the Mack truck twins. He threw me off, but that was kind of fun so I climbed on him again. The other truck twin was swatting at Dewey, who was sitting on his shoulders batting his head. I don't often say this, but — go, Dewey!

I saw other teams passing us, but if we couldn't win the race, I wanted to beat Sligo. I swam over to one of our canoe oars that was floating in the water. "Let's go," I yelled to Reese and Dewey.

Reese and Dewey let go of the other team and swam over to me. I held the oar across us, so Dewey and Reese could grab on. Then we started swimming, using the oar like a kickboard. With all three of us kicking it went really fast. We even passed some of the other canoes. The ones with teams that really didn't know how to row. We saw the finish line ahead of us. We crossed the line in second place, which is pretty amazing since we didn't have a canoe.

When they gave out the awards, Martin Stephen's team saluted us for the way we took care of Sligo. As Last of the Mohicans, they won kits to make your own moccasins. For coming in second, we won a free dinner at Natty Bumppo's, which served really excellent Bumppo Burgers. What were they thinking? We totally got the better prize.

After we got dried off, we all ate fried chicken at the picnic tables. Stevie's parents brought tofu in the shape of chicken, which they claimed was just as good. Yeah, right.

"So what happened?" my mom asked. "You were in the lead and then you all stood up and knocked the boat over. What'd you do that for?"

"Banana Joe attacked us!" said Reese. "He was hiding in Malcolm's knapsack!"

Stevie's eyes got wide. "I . . . thought . . . you . . . got . . . rid . . . of . . . him."

"We got rid of the wrong knapsack," I explained.

"Are you boys still trying to get rid of Dewey's monkey?" my mom demanded. "You know how much he likes it. It wasn't bad enough that you stuck him in the trash can outside our house?"

Reese and Dewey and I stared at her. "You know about that?" I asked.

"Of course I knew about it," Mom said. "Nothing gets by me. How did you think the monkey got back into your room? Did you think it got out of the garbage by itself?"

We looked at each other uncomfortably. We did kind of think that, but my mom didn't need to know about that.

"He can move by himself!" Dewey announced. "At night he watched me sleep. So I got out of bed, and I turned him so he was looking at Malcolm."

"You did that?" I yelled. Did he know how much sleep I had lost over that? "Anyway, he wasn't looking at you," I said. "I turned him so he was looking at Reese."

"You did that?" Reese yelled. "I turned him so he was looking at Dewey."

I did the math, figuring out exactly how many times Joe had gotten turned around from Dewey, to Reese, to me. Reese and Dewey listened carefully. But when I finished, we were still one turn short. "That one time," I said. "Joe must have moved on his own."

Dad reached over and took another wing. "I moved it once," he said casually.

"You did that?" Reese, Dewey, and I all yelled together. "Why?"

Dad shrugged. Mom started laughing.

"This isn't funny," said Reese.

"Oh, yes, it is," said Mom. "Look at the three of you! It took a stupid monkey to bring you together. You were all so busy trying to get one another, the monkey got you. But look what happened when you became a team."

We all looked at one another uncomfortably. I guess Mom was right.

"You were easy targets," Dad chuckled.

"So all those stories you told us about pitchforks and boys who didn't respect the monkey were made up?" I said.

"Oh, no, those were true," Dad said. "As far as I know."

Then he winked. What was that supposed to mean?

So it turned out Banana Joe was just a regular monkey who couldn't put a curse on anyone. He couldn't get out of the garbage can or into the canoe by himself. There was a logical explanation for everything that happened. Even Dewey admitted that he'd been playing with the glue the day we found him all stuck together.

"I like to pour it on my hands and peel it off when it's dry," he explained.

We never did figure out how Banana Joe got the Chiquita sticker onto the other knapsack. But now that it was gone, it didn't matter. I guess it's just part of the legend now. I had better things to think about.

Best of all, it was a great Survivor Day. I guess it wasn't such a bad thing after all that my mom put us all on the same team. Even Dewey turned out to be indispensable. I was kind of glad he'd blackmailed himself onto the team. Without Reese's hard head, Dewey's killer stickiness, Francis's lucky shark tooth, and my super rabbit powers, we never would have almost won. Most important, Sligo's team came in behind us with sixty-eight points.

I reached out to eat the last victory drumstick.

"Let go!" Reese yelled, tugging on the other end. "I went for it first!"

"You did not, moron!" I yelled.

Reese twisted the chicken leg around and tried to hit me on the head with it.

"Quit it!"

"Let go!"

We were still fighting over the chicken leg when Dewey climbed up on the table and took a bite out of it!

"You are so dead!" Reese shouted, still not letting go.

Dewey jumped off the table, and me and Reese ran after him, threatening him with the chicken leg.

Okay, so we weren't a team all the time. But we were there when we needed one another. I could live with that.

One more thing happened at Survivor Day. We were in the parking lot getting ready to leave. I saw Sligo and his parents walking toward their car. Sligo's parents look like bigger, meaner versions of him, by the way.

Sligo called me a wimp as he climbed into the backseat of his parents' car and they drove away. I started to yell something back, and then I stopped. It was sitting in Sligo's car, grinning out the back window.

Banana Joe.

Somehow Joe had made it to the Sligo station wagon.

Nobody knows how.

MALCOLM IN THE MIDDLE #4

THE EXCHANGE STUDENT

Is Malcolm's house big enough for two genius kids? That's the question when an exchange student from another school comes to live with his, uh, *unique,* family for one whole week.

The student is not what anyone was expecting.

First of all, he's a *she* — named Camellia.

Second of all, Camellia is every bit as smart as Malcolm.

Third of all, she's every bit as tough as Reese . . . as cute as Dewey . . . and, for the bonus round, Malcolm's mom and dad love her. She's the daughter they never had.

You don't have to be a genius to see that adds up to three strikes — she must be stopped.

Incoming: Here's a sneak preview of how Malcolm deals with the competition in *The Exchange Student*. You can read the rest of it by picking up the next book in the series, *Malcolm in the Middle: The Exchange Student,* in bookstores everywhere this February.

THE EXCHANGE STUDENT

EXCERPT

"No! No!" Dewey cried, trying to hold on to the threads in the rug. "She's going to get me!"

Reese and I looked at each other. She? It was embarrassing enough that Dewey was always being chased by imaginary monsters. If he was going to start being chased by female imaginary monsters . . . that was just too much.

We sat him up and pinned him against the bed. Reese pulled the lamp down from the night table and twisted it so the bulb shined right into Dewey's face. Dewey squirmed and tried to keep his eyes shut, but I held his head. I have no idea if this light in the face thing really works? But they always do it in cartoons when they want to make someone talk. It's pretty fun.

"Dewey, this is a three-way lightbulb," Reese said menacingly. He clicked it quickly through all three levels of brightness, then put it back on the lowest level. "We've got all day. We're going to break you."

That was my cue to play the good brother. "Dewey," I said. "Whatever it is, you can tell us. We just want to help you." Reese and I both smiled.

Dewey kicked and tried to escape, but it was hopeless. Finally, he started to talk. "I promised her I wouldn't tell," he said. "If I do she'll send her killer robot to get me!"

"Told on who?" I asked. "Who's got a killer robot?" If somebody in this house had a killer robot, I wanted to know about it.

"Camellia!" Dewey whispered. "She made me tell her things. She and her robot."

Reese frowned at me. "That exchange student?"

This was getting weird. "Dewey, what are you talking about?" I said.

Dewey took a couple of deep breaths. "I said I was going to tell on her. She said if I did her robot would come into my room at night and zap me with its laser eyes. Then it would twist my arms off and put me in the dishwasher."

Okay, it didn't take much for us to scare Dewey but we'd known him for life. I'd never seen anyone else find his panic buttons so fast.

Reese stuck his face right up to Dewey's. "Dewey, that's totally stupid. You don't even fit in the dishwasher, remember?"

That's when it hit me. Camellia might not have a killer robot like Dewey thought, but she had done something that Dewey could tell on her for. If Mom found out about it, Camellia could forget about taking over this family.

"Dewey," I said. "What did Camellia do that she doesn't want you to tell?"

Dewey shut his mouth and shook his head. Then he put his hands over his mouth. No matter how much Reese and I poked, shook, and threatened him, he wouldn't talk.

"I don't get it," said Reese. He looked a little worried. "How can he be more afraid of some girl than he is of me?" He cracked his knuckles for reassurance.

"Not only that," I said. "How could Camellia get Dewey so

scared he won't tell on her? We've been trying to keep him from telling on us since he learned to talk. Even Francis can't keep Dewey's mouth shut."

"It's weird," Reese said. "I always thought that if somebody figured out how to do it, it would be you. Camellia beat you to it."

"That's it," I said. "This ends now."

"GOTTA GET ON THE SET" SWEEPSTAKES

Win a trip to see a live taping of *Malcolm in the Middle*! As the Grand Prize winner, you and a friend will be whisked to California where you'll go behind the scenes of FOX's Emmy Award-winning show.

In addition, 50 First Prize winners will be awarded a prize package complete with a *Malcolm in the Middle* backpack, books based on the series, studio shots of the cast, and other surprises.

ENTER TODAY. JUST DEWEY IT!

How to Enter:

1. NO PURCHASE NECESSARY. To enter, download an official entry coupon at www.scholastic.com/titles/malcolm or hand print your name, address, birthdate, and telephone number on a 3" x 5" card and mail to: "Gotta Get on the Set" Sweepstakes, c/o Scholastic Inc., P.O. Box 7500, Jefferson City, MO 65101. Enter as often as you wish, one entry to an envelope. All entries must be postmarked between January 1, 2001 and April 1, 2001. Mechanically reproduced entries will not be accepted. Scholastic assumes no responsibility for lost, misdirected, damaged, stolen, postage-due, illegible, incomplete, or late entries. All entries become property of the sponsor and will not be returned.

2. Sweepstakes open to residents of the USA no older than 15 as of 12/31/2001, except employees of Scholastic, 20th Century Fox; Regency Entertainment (USA); and Monarchy Entertainment B.V. their respective affiliates, subsidiaries, respective advertising, promotion, and fulfillment agencies, and immediate families. Members of SAG and other professional acting groups also prohibited. Sweepstakes is void where prohibited by law.

3. Except where prohibited, by accepting the prize, winner consents to the use of his/her name, age, entry, and/or likeness by sponsors for publicity purposes without further compensation.

4. Winners will be selected at random by Scholastic Inc., whose decision is final with respect to all matters concerning this sweepstakes. Only one prize per winner. All winners will be notified by 5/30/2001, by Scholastic Inc. and all prizes will be awarded by before the close of the production season 2002. Odds of winning depend on the number of entries received. Winners and their legal guardians will be required to sign and return an affidavit of eligibility and liability release within 14 days of notification, or the prize will be forfeited.

5. Prizes: **Grand Prize**: 1 Grand Prize winner will win a trip for themselves, a friend and a parent/guardian to Los Angeles, California for 3 days and 2 nights. While in California, the winner and guests will visit the set of *Malcolm in the Middle* and watch a live taping of the show. Airline, hotel, meals and local transportation included. (Estimated retail value: $4,000) **1st Prize**: 50 First Prize winners will receive a *Malcolm in the Middle* prize package containing a set of *Malcolm in the Middle* books, studio photos, and other souvenir material from *Malcolm in the Middle*. (Estimated retail value: $45.00).

6. Prizes are non-transferable, not returnable, and cannot be sold or redeemed for cash. No substitution or transfer of prize allowed, except by Scholastic in the event of prize unavailability. Taxes on prizes are the responsibility of the winner. By accepting the prize, winner agrees that Scholastic Inc. and Fox, their respective officers, directors, agents and employees will have no liability or responsibility for any injuries, losses or damages of any kind resulting from and/or participation in this sweepstakes and they will be held harmless against any claims of liability arising directly or indirectly from acceptance, possession or use of any prize.

7. For list of winners, send a self-addressed stamped envelope after 06/01/2001 to: Malcolm in the Middle WINNERS, c/o Scholastic Inc., P.O. Box 7500, 2931 East McCarty Street, Jefferson City, MO 65101.